Jfic Sateren

CATon a hottie's tin roof

CAT on a hottie's tin roof

a novel by
Shelley Swanson Sateren

Delacorte Press

Published by
Delacorte Press
an imprint of
Random House Children's Books
a division of Random House, Inc.
New York

Visit us on the Web! www.randomhouse.com/kids

Educators and librarians, for a variety of teaching tools, visit us at
www.randomhouse.com/teachers

Library of Congress Cataloging-in-Publication Data
Sateren, Shelley Swanson.
Cat on a hottie's tin roof / Shelley Swanson Sateren.
p. cm.
Summary: Sixth-grader Cat tries to hide the fact that she is a good student in order to make friends with Cassidy, but when a third girl who likes the same music and fashions as Cassidy comes on the scene, Cat is afraid she will lose her new friend.
ISBN 0-385-73059-4 (trade)—ISBN 0-385-90088-0 (GLB)
[1. Friendship—Fiction. 2. Individuality—Fiction.] I. Title.
PZ7 .S249155 Cat 2003
[Fic]—dc21
2002013920

The text of this book is set in 11-point Dutch 801 Roman.
Book design by Angela Carlino
Printed in the United States of America
May 2003
BVG   10 9 8 7 6 5 4 3 2 1

For my parents, Steve and Judy,
my husband, Roald,
and my sons, Erik and Anders,
who always have a funny story to share

Bottomless gratitude to my editors, Diana Capriotti and Jodi Kreitzman, for their brilliant skill, great humor and belief in Cat.

Many thanks also to the people who contributed to the creation and publication of this book: Holly Bell; Shana Berg; Françoise Bui; Angela Carlino; Karl Fink; Beverly Horowitz; Emily Kidd; Hannah Longley; Kristen Olson; Tom Peine; Steve Swanson; Megan Thrasher; and Hannah Worku.

And heartfelt thanks to my two ultimate cheerleaders, Nancy Haugen Gaffey and Cheryl Michelsen Sletten; to Tennessee Williams for the title; and to my writing teacher, Judy Delton, in fond and loving memory.

✳ **Contents** ✳

1 Yummiest Harmonies Ever 1

2 Operation Nerd No More 11

3 Cute Band Alert 25

4 Secure Your Oxygen Masks 37

5 Whoa There, Buckaroos 49

6 Cat's Dog-Walking Service 58

7 Hot Pink Hair 70

8 Slurpable Pie 81

9 Psycho with a Capital *S* 95

10 Tiger Stripes and Leopard Spots 108

11 *C* for Cardiac Arrest 120

12 Pile of V.I.P. Passes 134

13 Hotel Sleuthhound 145

14 Descending the Tour Bus Steps 157

15 Preteen Private Eye 166

16 On the Hottie's Tin Roof 177

17 So Long, Babycakes 186

1

Yummiest Harmonies Ever

"**I**'ve e-mailed Annie seventeen times in four days, Mom, and *still* no answer from her!" I pointed at the blank computer screen with a limp wrist.

Mom shook her head and handed me a five-dollar bill. "Look, Cathy," she said. "You've moped for four days now. If you're not going to try to find a new friend, at least go to the store for me. We need a half dozen corn on the cob for dinner."

I gawked at her and blurted out, "Try to find a new friend . . . in my grade . . . at my school, Mom?" I *tsk*ed. "You know Lewis Elementary is filled with cliques so tight you couldn't crack them open with a jackhammer!"

Mom took my arm, led me downstairs, opened the front door and gently nudged me onto the porch.

"How about those two girls who live on Garr Street?" she asked. "The ones who wear cowboy boots?" She started to close the door on me.

I held it open and said, "Billie and Brooke. FYI, Mom, they're horse freaks. They're like two cowgirls joined at the chaps. They spend every free second at some ranch riding huge stallions or something—"

"Well, then," Mom interrupted, and continued firmly, "while you walk to QuikPick for me, think about another girl you might call. You're smart, Cathy. Put your cleverness to work." She smiled her discussion-is-over smile, peeled my fingers off the door and shut it on me.

I did a major huff and turned around, then trudged down Lucille Street Hill toward QuikPick.

As if being smart would help—that was precisely why I was in social crisis mode! Way back in first grade, Annie and I got blacklisted as brainiacs and the nerd label had stuck like glue ever since. No kids besides Annie ever stooped to speak to me. But now Annie's family had moved to Paris, and my one and only friend in the cosmic universe was gone! Sixth grade was starting in just ten short days—how could I face it alone?

I sighed and sulked on. It was super-hot, humid and windy out. Typical for the last week in August in the Twin Cities metro. Yuck. My limp, stringy hair kept flying in my face and mini–dust devils blew out of the gutter and managed to blast under my wire-rim glasses. I was sure I looked like a total nerd—and that's when it hit me: Greg Twitchell.

He was the only other kid at Lewis Elementary who actually talked to me. Greg, Annie and I were tied for top student/top nerd status at our school. He always had his head bent over an encyclopedia or calculator, but sometimes he'd look up when I walked past his desk and say things like "How many extra-credit points did you get? I bet you did great."

My old holey tennies slowed to a stop. I turned around and headed away from QuikPick. I'd take a detour to the store . . . by way of Martin Avenue.

I knew Greg lived there. Once I'd seen him fixing his bicycle chain in front of a red house with white trim.

Maybe Greg and I could eat lunches together in the cafeteria, so I wouldn't have to sit alone in that big creepy room. It wouldn't be as good as having a girlfriend, but at least it was a start.

I marched up three long city blocks and found the red house. Hiding behind an old oak tree on the boulevard, I stood on tiptoe, trying to conduct a little espionage. But a row of bushes totally obscured my view.

I scaled the trunk of the oak tree to get a better view. I wound my arms and legs tightly around a thick branch, then peeked through the leaves. There was no sign of life in the yard or in the windows.

"Drat. Maybe he's not home," I whispered to myself, squinting through the thick leaves whipping about in the high wind. My glasses slid down my hot, sweaty nose. I pushed them back up and squinted some more.

Suddenly a bike zipped by on the sidewalk and pulled into the Twitchells' driveway. I pushed a mass of green leaves out of my face, and now I had a clear bird's-eye view of my egghead classmate.

Greg hopped off his bike, and I gasped quietly. He'd grown so much over the summer! I'd always towered over all the boys at Lewis Elementary. But now it looked like a boy had caught up to me in height. Finally!

FYI, for as long as I'd known Greg, his button-down-collar shirts always hung half in/half out of his wrinkled khakis. And for years he'd had too-long ringlets that dangled past the bridge of his nose like a shaggy dog's. You couldn't see his eyes at all.

Now Greg had the same sheepdog hair, but it was sun-bleached and extra curly from the humidity. His skin was slightly tan and he wore wrinkled khaki shorts instead of long pants. For a split second Greg Twitchell actually looked . . . *cute.*

I had climbed farther out on the branch to get a better vista of the boyscape when a big gust of wind shook my perch. My fingers slipped, I tumbled sideways . . . and plunged toward the ground.

Suddenly, whump. A hard yank at the back of my neck stopped me midtumble. The strap of my bib overalls caught on a branch. My glasses bounced off my sweaty nose and landed on the grass.

I tried to shake myself loose. Ooomph. I flailed my arms and legs. No luck. I was stranded, my holey tennies dangling four feet off the ground.

Exactly 2.2 seconds later, Greg leaped over. "Cathy?" he said. "Cathy Carlson? What are you doing in that tree?"

Gulp. "I'm, uh . . . branching out," I squeaked.

Greg laughed. Good sign! I'd always managed to make Annie laugh too.

"Actually, Greg, I'm caught on a branch."

"Oh, a damsel in distress. Here, I'll help." Greg cupped his palms together and gave me a foothold. I stood on his hand and he boosted me up, high enough to release my overalls strap. It popped free and I dropped—right into Greg's arms.

I lay there for five full seconds, too shocked to hop to my feet.

I learned a lot from the smartest boy in sixth grade during those five seconds. I learned how strong his arms were. I'd never known he had strong arms. I learned how easily he blushed, too. His face turned bright red. But the most fascinating fact I learned was this: Greg Twitchell had huge, beautiful blue eyes. A powerful gust of wind blew the thatch of hair off his forehead, and for the first time ever I caught a glimpse of the top half of Greg's face. He tilted his head and a late-afternoon sun ray beamed right into his peepers and turned them aquamarine.

Apparently Greg noticed mine just then, too, probably because my glasses had flown off my face. "You have really green eyes, Cathy," he said quietly, and blushed a deeper shade of red. "I've never noticed them before. Your emerald irises would match everything in the city of Oz."

Suddenly my joints turned to oatmeal. I was pure dead weight now. Too much for Greg to hold another second. He set me down gently on the grass.

I grabbed my glasses off the boulevard and wiped the dirt off them with my T-shirt.

"Uh, I—I have to go, Cathy," Greg stammered, his hair falling back over his eyes. "I'm late for my mom's birthday dinner." He loped across his lawn and disappeared into the house.

My mouth hung open. I reached up and pushed under my chin to close it, and headed to QuikPick in a daze. Greg had been hiding sapphires under that furry fringe all these years. I doubted anybody but me at our school knew about his gem-stones. And he seemed to like mine too. Unbelievable! No one in my school, except Annie, seemed to like anything about me. Maybe sixth grade would be all right after all.

That's when I remembered Judd the Jerk, a boy in our class with a mean streak a mile wide. Ugh. I could just hear him jeer, "Greg and Cathy aren't lovebirds, they're love-*nerds*!" Besides, it might be hard being friends with someone you had a little . . . crush on. Especially if that feeling was maybe, just maybe . . . mutual.

I trudged into QuikPick and toward the vegetable section.

I had grabbed six ears of corn and was headed toward the checkout counter when I stopped dead in my tracks.

A girl with a huge head of ultra-frizzy hair stood at the magazine stand with her face buried deep in a copy of *Sizzle Pop*. Her curls were held behind her ears with a billion cute sparkly barrettes every color of the rainbow. She wore funky yellow flip-flops with plastic daisies on top, honeydew-green glitter shorts and a polka-dot tank. This girl looked like a splash of pure summer style.

I glanced down at my ancient crusty overalls. Mom had bought them at Savers Plus back when I was in fourth grade. She'd offered to get me new ones, but they were so comfortable I begged her to let out the straps every summer, and they still fit me, more or less. I'd never noticed what they looked like before, but now I saw the driblets of spaghetti sauce and lime sherbet from dinner the night before speckled on the front. Aaargh. Even though my clothes were all food-splattered, I knew I was no fashion plate.

I grabbed the August issue of *Tween: Back-to-Cool* and pretended to study the models prancing across the pages in their plaid minis and matching backpacks. I peeked at the frizzy-haired girl. Who was she anyhow? Her nose was stuck so deep in *Sizzle Pop* that I couldn't see her face. Granted, this wasn't the best outfit to wear to meet someone so stylish, but if she was new to the neighborhood, maybe she wouldn't mind and my friendship troubles would be over!

I waited for her to look up from the music scene magazine. It felt like practically five whole minutes passed. The girl kept staring at the very same page. My feet started to fall asleep.

Finally I took a chance and said, "Hi! I'm Cathy Carlson."

The girl raised her head and looked over at me. She gave me a super-warm smile.

Holy moly. A nice smile from a girl my age. This was *not* normal. And hey, I knew her! I mean, I recognized her. She was in my grade at Lewis Elementary! I thought she'd transferred to our school the past spring. She had been in one of the other fifth-grade classes, so I didn't know her name or anything about her.

"I go to your school." I smiled back.

"Hi! I'm Cassidy McDew." She grinned. "Hey, I have a cousin named Cathy but her nickname is Cat. As in meow. Is that your nickname too?"

I shook my head and had a late-afternoon fingernail snack.

"Too bad," Cassidy said. "Cat is a cool name."

Cathy wasn't cool, obviously. My shoulders drooped. Nothing about me was cool. Even my name was boring!

I watched Cassidy reach down and straighten the sassy plastic daisy on her left flip-flop. I thought with a sigh, How could I have ever thought this fashionable girl would like anything about me? I'd just have to spend the year alone, sitting in the bathroom stall during lunch to avoid being teased in the cafeteria. Gross! I'd get indigestion eating my tuna sandwiches that close to a toilet. A whole year of heartburn and an upset stomach! Unless . . .

"Look, Cassidy, you can call me Cat, okay?" I said.

"Fab!" Cassidy's smile could melt ice cream, I swear.

A gush of pride pumped through my veins. I had a cool new name! This couldn't be happening!

The next second I was fishing for some necessary information. "Um, I was in 5A last year, Cassidy," I said. "Were you in 5B or 5C?"

"5C."

"Oh. Did you, um, make many friends there?"

Cassidy shook her moptop. "Seems like everybody's already paired off as BFFs at that Lewis Elementary," she said matter-of-factly. "I guess that figures, by fifth grade."

Oh, what luck! Cassidy McDew had discovered that our school was Clique City and she felt like Outcast Girl too! I said excitedly, "So you know that a girl on the periphery can sure feel rebuffed, right?"

"Huh?" Cassidy wrinkled up her nose and giggled.

Oops. "Uh, never mind. It doesn't matter." Maybe I couldn't talk like a dictionary around Cassidy McDew. That old habit would be hard to break. Annie and I had always played verbal volleyball, flinging long hard words at each other for fun.

Suddenly Cassidy held up her copy of *Sizzle Pop.* "I can't take my eyeballs off him," she sighed, showing me a full-page photo of a pop star. "Milo Lennox. Don't you just love him? I just love love love his new hit single, 'Me and You Like School Glue.' Every time I play the CD or the song comes on the radio, I pass out cold."

"I haven't heard that song," I admitted, glancing at the picture of Milo Lennox. I'd never paid any attention to pop music. It was an alien world to me. All the radios at our house (all two of them) were tuned to public radio exclusively.

Cassidy gawked at me and squeaked, "You haven't *heard* 'Like School Glue'? You're kidding! It's always on KDQB!"

Double oops. What in heck did I go and admit that for? I wished I could suck that slipup right back down my throat.

"Well, you *have* to hear it," Cassidy said firmly. "You will die. The Milo Lennox Band has the yummiest harmonies I've ever heard. They're really good dancers, too. I bought the *School Glue* CD. Wanna come over to my house and hear it?"

My heart skipped a beat. "To your house?" I said. "Right now?"

Cassidy nodded fast, her eyes twinkling as brightly as her glitter shorts.

"Yes!"

2

Operation
Nerd No More

"**A**nnie is from the serious tribe," my little sister, Lizzie, often said.

I thought about that as Cassidy made goofy faces at QuikPick's surveillance camera. We were standing in line, waiting to pay. Never in a billion years would Annie have done that. Then again, last year Annie memorized one of Shakespeare's sonnets and recited it to the whole school assembly on Teacher Appreciation Day, which I thought was beyond brave.

I paid for the corn, borrowed QuikPick's phone and asked Mom if I could go to Cassidy's. "Are her parents home?" Mom asked over the line.

I held the receiver away from my ear and asked Cassidy.

She twirled one of her frizzy locks around her finger, her head tilted sweetly, and replied, "My dad's gone for five weeks this time. He's a trucker. My mom's working at the mall and my big brother, Baird, is working at the auto body shop. But my great-granny Rose is home. Plus I have a watchdog. Tell your mom we'll be safe, Cat. Puff is ferocious."

Mom heard Cassidy say all that. "Okay, honey," Mom replied. "But it's already four o'clock now. Please be home in half an hour so we can start dinner. Workshops start for me tomorrow and I want to get to bed early."

I barely heard her. "Okay, bye, Mom," I mumbled, and hung up the phone. Drat. Why did Cassidy have to have a watchdog? Now I was afraid to hang out at her house.

We headed up Murray Street to Cassidy's. My heart beat a little faster with each step. Was her watchdog a Doberman? Or—double drat—a bull terrier? I could see the sharp teeth bared now, taking a nice big bite out of my leg.

"Here's my place," Cassidy said. "I mean, my great-grandma's. We live with her now." The McDews' house sat next to the railroad tracks, three blocks from our school. As Cassidy reached for the doorknob, I yelped, "No! Don't let Puff out, Cassidy. Please!"

Cassidy's round hazel eyes filled with concern. "Don't be afraid of my cat, Dog. I mean, don't be afraid of my dog, Cat." She giggled at her mistake. "He won't hurt you, I promise."

Cassidy threw open the front door. I had turned to run

when the tiniest little gray puffball bounced out onto the front porch.

"*This* is your watchdog?" I laughed. Phew! "I thought you said he was ferocious."

"I was kidding." Cassidy giggled and grabbed the bouncy fluffball. "Want to hold him?" She put Puff in my arms.

"Oh, he's so soft," I breathed. Instantly, Puff went limp in my arms. "Is he made of butter?" I asked. "He's melting."

Cassidy laughed. Excellent!

"Oh, he loves you, Cat! Look, he's so relaxed. It's like he's at a doggie spa in your arms. You're a dog lover like me, Cat, aren't you?"

"You bet!" I'd never known I was a dog-loving Cat before that moment. Fine by me. Two more friendship points for sure!

"Do you like his rhinestone collar?" Cassidy asked. "I made it."

"You did?" I gushed, eyeing the green and blue rhinestones.

"Yup. My mom works at Craft Barn at the mall. She got me a glue gun, rhinestones and glitter. Everything's half price with her discount."

"Lucky!" I couldn't imagine my mom ever working there. Shopping malls gave her massive headaches.

Cassidy led me inside the house. She peeked into the McDews' living room.

"Great-granny Rose is taking a nap," she whispered. "Follow me, Cat."

We tiptoed through the living room, past the couch where Cassidy's great-grandma was sleeping. The old woman's skin was super-pale. Her hair was long and pure white. She lay on her back, straight and stiff, her bony arms crossed over her chest like she was . . . eek.

We sprang quietly up the stairs and darted into Cassidy's room. Then my eyes nearly popped out of my head.

"Wow!" I exclaimed, totally shocked. Every square millimeter of Cassidy's bedroom walls *and* ceiling was covered with photos of celebrities.

"Most are pictures of the Milo Lennox Band," Cassidy said proudly. She got busy with her pointer finger. "There's Milo, holding his cool yellow guitar. . . . That's Duke the drummer. . . . That's Jarvis the piano player. . . . Those guys are the backup singers. . . . And those girls are the backup dancers. I have two hundred and fifty-seven posters and pictures of the Milo Lennox Band in all. And now," she said, wiggling her new copy of *Sizzle Pop* in the air, "I'll have two hundred and sixty-one." Cassidy grabbed a pair of scissors off her dresser and got busy clipping. "Isn't he de*lish*? Milo is such a hottie, my heart stops every time I look at him."

"That must be often in this room." I laughed.

"Yup." Cassidy giggled. She was a complete giggle machine. I'd just love to have a total laugh factory for a friend, I thought.

Puff flopped onto the carpet and started to pant. It was super-warm in Cassidy's room.

I wiped my sweaty forehead and stepped over to Cassidy's shelves. They were covered with fashion and music magazines. I picked up a copy of *Sizzle Pop* and thumbed through it. "Do you, um, have lots of friends from your old hometown, Cassidy?" I asked, slyly checking out the competition in the comrade department.

"Not really," she replied, cutting out another photo. "Before we moved here, we lived in Iowa, but not for long. And not long in North Dakota or Kansas before that, either."

"So you're a new kid in schools a lot."

"Too much. I hate sitting alone in the caf."

Oh, this was great news! Not Cassidy's lonesomeness, of course, but her needing me at lunchtimes, too! "My friend Annie just moved to France," I said quietly. "She'll be a new kid in a new country."

"That would be double hard," said Cassidy. "Maybe *we* can sit together this year."

"Good idea!" I said, barely able to contain my excitement.

Then she dropped the scissors on her dresser and pressed a button on her CD player. Cassidy turned the volume on low and Milo's "Me and You Like School Glue" filled the room.

"I don't want to blast it," she said, swaying to the beat. "That might wake up Great-granny Rose and scare her."

Scare her to death, I thought.

Cassidy kept dancing in place. "Don't they rock?" she asked.

"Um—yeah," I lied. "They're metamorphic for sure." The

guitars twanged, the singers whined and the drums banged way too loudly, even with the volume on low. And the lyrics were as corny as the cobs I'd just bought at QuikPick. "Don't make me blue . . . Show me you love me too . . . I'm stuck on you, like school glue . . . Yooo hooo . . . ," Milo sang. Annie and I never listened to music like this. She was a violin virtuoso and only liked classical.

We met in Baby Mozart class at Orchestra Hall when we were six months old. In our eleven years of best friendship, I never once saw Annie tune her radio to KDQB. It was strictly Bach and Beethoven over her radio waves, just like mine.

Mom always insisted on soothing classical music to calm her nerves, especially after her long days of teaching high school English. And I kind of liked lyric-free music when I was reading a book. It was less distracting that way.

But what did I know? If Milo was the latest tidal wave, then maybe I had to learn to surf—especially if I wanted to hang out with Cassidy.

"I heard on KDQB that Milo's going on tour soon. He might come to the Twin Cities!" Cassidy bopped her hips and snapped her fingers. "Isn't that just so *fab*?"

"Right," I offered. "Totally fab."

Cassidy was bopping in top gear now. She looked like a flag in a high wind, flapping her arms and swaying her legs like crazy. Standing still, I felt like the flagpole.

"I'll be first in line to buy a ticket," Cassidy went on. "I've got a hundred dollars saved from all the cuts and curls I did for everybody in my family this year. I even cut my brother's and dad's hair. They pay me three bucks, and Great-granny Rose pays me five bucks for a shampoo and set. I've even done colors for my mom and aunt." She grabbed her piggy bank off her shelf and shook it as she danced. "Oink. Oink. My bank is fat with cash. Pretty good, huh?"

"Yeah! Wow, you're a real hairdresser?" I asked.

"Yup. Do you want a new do? I love trying out new looks." Cassidy stopped dancing, took my arm and led me over to her desk. My jaw dropped. A gazillion hairbrushes, combs and mirrors lay jumbled among a trillion jars and bottles of hair spray and mysterious hair goops.

Cassidy nudged me toward the desk chair. "Here, sit down."

"I don't know. . . ." I was used to my dirty-dishwater-blond hair hanging in limp strings. I'd had that look for eleven years.

"C'mon!" Cassidy giggled.

"I don't think so." I stared uncomfortably at all those beauty products on the desktop. I'd never been to a beauty shop in my life. To save cash, Mom always cut Lizzie's and my hair.

Cassidy picked up a few strings of my hair and studied them. "If it's money you're worried about—"

"Yes! Money!" I blurted out, ready to bolt out of that chair. "You see, my dad is a professor and he's on sabbatical this year—"

"Where's that?" Cassidy asked.

Cripes. I definitely had to stop talking like a dictionary

around Cassidy. "Uh, my dad gets half paychecks for the whole school year. So my family's on a tight budget—"

"Gotcha. I won't charge you a penny, because you're a friend."

A friend? My heart leaped. That made me so happy I shut my mouth in a millisecond.

Cassidy grabbed a hairbrush and brushed my limp-linguini hair away from my face. "You're super-sweaty, Cat," she said. "I'll give you a whale-spout updo. That'll get all this hair off your neck."

"Well, okay," I said, and winced. Granted, maybe I needed an updated look to help hide my inner nerd. But this was all so sudden. I felt like I was on a collision course in fashion orbit. If only Cassidy's desk chair had a seat belt.

Cassidy brushed my hair straight up and secured it tightly with about ten rubber band thingamabobs. A super-tall ponytail stuck straight out from the top of my head, like a torpedo. I gulped. Then Cassidy grabbed a can of hair spray. She squirted and squirted until the tail was totally stick-uppy, completely unassisted. I'd never known my hair was capable of doing that.

Then Cassidy squirted some more.

I coughed like crazy. When the cloud of spray cleared, I gave the petrified geyser a pat.

"Wow," I muttered. "It feels like a *rock*."

"I knew you'd love it!" Cassidy gushed. "It's super-cute on you, Cat. I love funky styles!"

"Me too," I lied. I had no idea what hairstyles I loved, for Pete's sake. "Thanks, Cassidy."

I stood up slowly, feeling a little off balance with that shellacked boulder on my scalp. Annie would die if she saw it. But she wasn't here anymore; only Cassidy was. . . .

Suddenly I spied the little lime-green clock on Cassidy's nightstand: 4:45! "I have to get this corn to my mom, Cassidy. Do you want to come to my house for dinner?" I asked.

"Yeah!" Cassidy looked pleased out of her gourd! "I'll ask Great-granny. Let's go see if she's awake. But first—" Cassidy grabbed a makeup bag off her desktop and got busy smearing on blue eye shadow. "Want to borrow some, Cat?"

Gulp. "Maybe tomorrow," I fibbed. Mom didn't allow Lizzie and me to wear makeup. "Never be a victim of Madison Avenue," my mom always said.

Just then a bunch of loud yelps and thumps came from downstairs. Oh no! Was Great-granny Rose . . . in trouble?

Cassidy and I dashed out to the hallway and peered through the banisters. From above, we spied Great-granny Rose whacking the couch pillows with her cane. She pointed a crooked finger at a blaring black-and-white TV and shouted, "You stay away from Jerome! He's my peach!"

Cassidy giggled. "It's Great-granny's favorite soap," she whispered in my ear. "*True Love at Twilight.* She's in love with the star. She's just jealous because the soap queen Modesty wants to marry him."

"Oh!" Whew. Great-granny Rose was okay.

"Better not to disturb her now," Cassidy whispered. "I'll just leave a note for Mom. She'll be home soon. Come on, Cat!"

* * *

At our house, Mom, Dad and my nine-year-old sister, Lizzie, gawked when they saw my new hairdo. They were completely speechless.

"Isn't Cassidy gifted with a hairbrush and a bottle of hair spray?" I said forcefully. Do not make *any* funny remarks and hurt my new friend's feelings, I pleaded silently.

Still no response from my tongue-tied family.

"They're just awestruck," I whispered reassuringly to Cassidy.

Finally, Mom clapped her hands together. "Well! Let's get ready for dinner, shall we? Please set an extra place for Cassidy, Cathy."

"Call me Cat, Mom. My old name is in the archives." Oops. Maybe *archive* was a brainiac word. I glanced at Cassidy, but she was looking at the family photos on our piano. I didn't think she heard my vocabulary slipup. Whew.

"You want us to call you . . . Cat?" Mom asked.

Lizzie said, "Do you mean cat, as in cheetah, jaguar, lion, tiger, Siamese, Persian—"

"Yes!" I interrupted impatiently. "I will respond only to Cat from now on, thank you."

"But cats never respond when you call them anything," Dad said in typical professor mode.

"True, but beside the point," I replied. "Can we eat now, please?"

"Just as soon as the food is done, Cathy—I mean, Cat," Mom replied, and smiled politely. Wide-eyed, she took the bag of corn from me, then she and Dad disappeared into the kitchen. Lizzie trailed along behind them, saying, "Here, kitty, kitty" as she left the room.

Cassidy was still looking at all our pictures. Right behind the piano, I noticed with sudden panic, were our living room bookshelves. They covered the whole wall from floor to ceiling and sagged with millions of thick books. Yikes. I hadn't seen a single book at Cassidy's house. What would she say if she saw all of ours? She clearly wasn't a bookworm.

I quickly jumped in front of Cassidy, to block her view. I was a lot taller than she was, so that seemed to work. I guided her into the dining room and over to the table.

"Here, Cassidy," I said, "take this seat! It's got the comfiest cushion of all the chairs!" Actually, it was the only one that had no direct view of any books in our house.

"I feel like a princess at your place!" Cassidy said with a grin, and plopped her butt down.

Five minutes later, we'd all barely begun to eat when Dad said, "My wife tells me your father is a trucker, Cassidy. What's his destination this trip?"

Cassidy swallowed a mouthful of fried chicken, then replied, "I think he's driving to Seattle in Washington, D.C."

Lizzie's eyebrows went up. FYI, my sister was a geography

freak. She loved every subject, but geography the most. She memorized world capitals and national currencies and gross national products just for fun. Lizzie put down her napkin and scooted to the edge of her seat.

I shot her a look. It said, "Don't you dare run and get the atlas and drag it in here and turn this into a teaching moment. If you do, Cassidy will be *so* embarrassed and we'll look like the egghead family."

Lizzie could see I meant business. She kept her trap shut and stayed put on her chair.

I breathed easier and finished my chicken without choking.

After dinner I rushed Cassidy through the living room, then hauled her upstairs, careful to shut the study door so she couldn't see the mountain of books in there. "Can you wait out here for a tiny second?" I asked, then darted ahead of Cassidy into my room. I yanked my blanket off my bed and chucked it over my bookshelf.

"Come on in, Cassidy," I said enthusiastically, and she stepped inside.

That was when I noticed, for the first time in my life, that my walls were . . . barren. All I had were some watercolor pictures I'd painted, my spelling bee winner certificates and photos of me performing in piano recitals. In contrast to Cassidy's room, with more than 261 pictures of superstars, my room looked like dullsville. Zzzzzz. I made a mental note: Buy a Milo Lennox Band poster ASAP.

Cassidy stepped over to my dresser. She fingered my agate

and pinecone collections, then my stones from the north shore of Lake Superior. "Where's all your makeup?" she asked.

Uh-oh. "My sister must've borrowed it," I lied. Even my mom didn't own a speck of makeup. Her daily "beauty" regimen was soap and water.

Suddenly I spied the stack of encyclopedias and dictionaries (including my new French-English one) on my nightstand. Oh no! Those reference books had *nerd* written all over them!

I quickly grabbed the books, threw open my closet door and dumped them way in the back, behind my shoes and snow boots.

I whirled around. Whew! Cassidy hadn't seen my quick paw work. She was carefully examining a giant prickly pinecone.

She turned toward me and her gaze landed on the clothes hanging in my closet. "Have you finished your school-clothes shopping?" she asked. "I'm all done. I have six cute new outfits." She stepped over and started to thumb through my hangers.

I chewed my lip. All I had were two pairs of non-designer jeans from Savers Plus, a few nature-lover tees from the science museum gift shop (bought with our family membership discount, before it expired in July) and a pile of sweaters in boring greens and browns.

Cassidy finished thumbing through my clothes, then turned around and yawned. Great. My wardrobe was putting her to sleep, just like I'd suspected. I sighed and admitted,

"Actually, Cassidy, I'm done shopping too. My family's on that tight budget this year."

"Too bad." Cassidy sat down on the edge of my bed. "But hey, I know where to clothes-shop on a budget! You could get some super-cool things for super-cheap. It's a used-clothing store called Resurrection Duds."

My heart did three cartwheels. "I've still got this week's allowance," I said excitedly. "That's five bucks. And I've got ten dollars of Christmas money left."

"Fan-*tas*-tic!" said Cassidy. "I love to pick out glam outfits. Let's go tomorrow!"

"I can't wait!" I bounced on the toes of my holey tennies. Tomorrow, I'd give my image an overhaul. I'd call it Operation Nerd No More. I never wanted Cassidy McDew to look in my closet and feel the slightest urge to yawn again. I had to hurry and peel off my nerdgirl label before Cassidy caught on to the truth.

3

Cute Band Alert

"**O**ld Faithful has lost its uppity-do," I muttered to myself, gazing in the mirror Monday morning. My new look hadn't survived the night. The ponytail stuck out from the side of my head now instead of the top. But I couldn't dismantle the droopy tail, because this was the hairdo that Cassidy had chosen for me. And it was the closest thing to *cool* I'd ever worn on my scalp!

I trudged to the study in my pj's and checked my e-mail. Still no word from Annie. What in heck was she *doing* in Paris, for Pete's sake? She'd promised she'd keep in touch.

Back in my room, I tugged on my old boring farmer bibs for the last time. Today I'd buy some new cool clothes, then buh-bye to Granola Girl and hello, style! I headed downstairs with a spring in my step.

Lizzie sat across the kitchen table, putting together a metal model of the solar system. She looked up and gazed at my floppy ponytail. "You look like a rabbit with one ear missing, Cat." She added Jupiter to the solar system, then said, "I saw on the school calendar that class lists are posted today—"

"Oh! That's right!" I wolfed down my cereal, then ran outside to get my weekly allowance from Dad. He was in the alley, tinkering with the Volvo engine. He pulled a five out of his wallet with oily fingers and said, "Spend that money wisely, Cath—I mean, Cat. We're really tightening the purse strings this year. That five dollars needs to last you all week."

"I know, Dad. Don't worry. Wisdom is my middle name."

Dad laughed and turned back to his greasy oil filter.

I scrambled back inside, looked up Rose McDew in the St. Paul white pages, then, presto, rang up Cassidy. "Cassidy, hi! It's me, Cat," I said. "We have to check out the class lists before we go to Resurrection Duds, okay? Let's meet at school in fifteen minutes. Cross your fingers that we get into the same class!"

"I'll cross everything," she replied. "My fingers, legs and eyes. Wish hard, Cat!"

I did. And all our wishing worked! Soon Cassidy and I were at Lewis Elementary skimming the class lists posted in the hallway and I was crying, "There we are! We're both in 6A!"

Cassidy screamed and grabbed my hand in a tight squeeze, like we were old friends. I was having happiness palpitations!

We calmed down and studied the class lists more closely. Greg Twitchell's name jumped out at me next. He was in our class too! Excellent. I could keep an eye on my secret crush all year.

Then I spied a name on the 6A list that I didn't recognize. "Shana Fitz," I read aloud. "Who's that?"

"That'd be me," we heard a voice behind us say.

Cassidy and I whirled around. A long-haired girl wearing leather pants stood behind us.

Cassidy gasped and marched right up to Shana Fitz. "I'm Cassidy and I *love* your cowhide pants," she gushed. "I wish I had some."

My heart sank. Cassidy hadn't loved any of the clothes in my closet.

"Thanks." Shana shrugged, as if she were used to getting compliments every hour of her life. "I had to wear them for my first trip to school. But I'm boiling." She eyed Cassidy's pink tank top and side-zippered mini appreciatively. "I can see people know how to dress cool here." Then her gaze landed on my crusty bibs. "Well, I guess some people do," she muttered, and wrinkled her nose.

Drat! Cassidy and I should have gone to Resurrection Duds *before* coming to school!

Then Shana spied my lopsided ponytail and laughed.

"What happened to you?" she asked. "Did you stick your head in a toilet and give yourself a swirly?"

I withered on the spot. I looked at Cassidy for backup, since the hairdo that Shana Fitz had just insulted was her creation. But Cassidy was still mesmerized by those tight buckskins. Her eyes weren't moving off them.

I did a fake chuckle and changed the subject. "Did you move?" I asked. "Or transfer?"

"Transferred. I got kicked out of Catholic school," Shana replied matter-of-factly.

"Oh!" I said, shocked. "That's too bad."

"No it isn't," Shana replied with a snort. "I'm *glad*."

My mouth fell open. If this girl hated school as much as it seemed, I'd really have to hide the fact that I liked it.

"Finally," Shana went on, her hands on her hips, "I can wear clothes I like to school *and* listen to my Discman at recess, I hope!" She *tsk*ed and rolled her eyes.

"What music do you like to listen to?" Cassidy asked eagerly.

"Right now the Milo Lennox Band is my fave—"

"You're kidding! Me too!" Cassidy squealed. "They rock!"

"I know," Shana said. "I *looove* their new video. And Milo's so cute it's sick, but the best thing about that band is their dancing. They have totally killer choreography. I've got the dance moves to 'Me and You Like School Glue' memorized."

"You *do*?" Cassidy yelped.

"Yup. To all of his songs, actually. I taped his 'Live From Orlando' TV concert off cable and I've played it a trillion times. I've learned practically every step." Suddenly Shana started bopping right there in the school hallway.

"You have Milo's TV concert *on tape*?" Cassidy's eyes opened super-wide.

I began to devour a fingernail. Cassidy hadn't gotten this excited over anything I'd said the day before.

"Sure," Shana replied. "All two hours of it."

"Ohhhhh, you are sooooo lucky," Cassidy said, exhaling dramatically. "We don't have cable at my great-grandma's house."

"Me neither," I peeped, wanting to make myself heard, even if it was just a few syllables.

Nobody seemed to notice.

"Two whole hours of Milo on video." Cassidy sighed. "That would be like heaven."

"Do you wanna come over and watch it?" Shana asked Cassidy. "I have to go home and change anyhow. I'm sweating like a pig."

I stuck a loose piece of hair into my mouth and sucked on it nervously. Shana hadn't asked me to come over, only Cassidy.

"Cool!" Cassidy said. "I'd *love* to see that concert."

Shana nudged Cassidy's arm and the two headed for the door. I stood alone in the school hallway, my bony shoulders falling into a slump. "Um, hey, can I come too?" I called, trying not to let my voice sound too quivery.

Cassidy turned and said, "Oh, sorry, Cat!" Then she asked Shana, "Can Cat come too?"

Shana glanced back and studied my whole beanpole body, from my stringy hair down to my knobby knees. I felt like a fly-covered hot dog in the school cafeteria—and Shana was the grossed-out girl in the lunch line. Suddenly, combating nerd syndrome felt overwhelmingly hopeless to me.

But just then Shana made a *W* with her fingers and said, "What*ever*."

I was invited! I jumped and ran after them. I trotted along behind Shana and Cassidy, across the schoolyard and up Carrey Street, a fake smile plastered on my face.

"I heard on MTV he broke up with that super-slimy supermodel Persephone," Shana said authoritatively. "Thank God."

"I saw in *Sizzle Pop* his favorite cereal is Cap'n Crunch. I eat it every morning for breakfast now," Cassidy said.

"He's a Taurus. No wonder he's so talented," Shana said.

"He owns eight Harley-Davidsons. I wish he'd give me a ride," Cassidy said wistfully.

I listened to them jabber on and on about Milo Lennox and for the first time in my life I felt about as bright as a snuffed-out candle.

Just then Shana looked at me and demanded, "What's your favorite song on his new album?"

I gulped. "Uh . . . 'Like School Glue'?" I peeped.

"Second fave?"

Oh no! I was about to flunk a pop culture pop quiz right in front of these guys! Suddenly my face flared up. The temperature outside was at least in the high eighties, but with my face all aflame it felt like 120 degrees.

Cassidy said sweetly, "Well, *my* second fave is 'Goddess Caffeina.' "

"Me too!" Shana chimed in. She started to sing and Cassidy joined her. "Pour me up a double cream and sugar latte . . . You behind the counter at the Java Jolt café . . . Goddess Caffeina . . . Sweet Goddess Caffeina . . . I'm only drinking up your beauty today . . . Forgetting all about my café au lait . . . Goddess Caffeina . . . Sweet Goddess Caffeina . . ."

I tagged along, totally mute, wishing I could sing along with them. I just had to memorize Milo's songs super-soon!

"There's my house." Shana pointed at a big sprawling new house with a fancy front door. A white Jeep Wrangler was parked in the driveway.

"Oh, I *love* Jeeps! They're so *cute,*" Cassidy cooed.

Hmmm. She didn't say that about the two rusty old Volvos in my driveway.

"And I *love* your house, Shana," Cassidy added.

"My dad's company built it. He's in construction."

"We live three blocks from each other." Cassidy was all bubbles and beaming grins. "We can walk to school together."

"School. Yuck." Shana scrunched up her face. "Don't remind me."

Cassidy giggled. Uh-oh. Did she wrinkle up her nose at the idea of school too? I gnawed on another fingernail.

If Shana and Cassidy walked to school together every day and home again at three-thirty, they'd get *thisclose,* and I'd be the lonely egghead left on the fringe.

I quickly scooted up to Cassidy and said quietly out the side of my mouth, "Can we go to Resurrection Duds now? Please?"

Cassidy waved her hand and said happily, "Let's just watch Milo's concert first, okay, Cat? Then we can go shopping."

But I needed those cooler clothes right that minute! And not because of the temperature!

"How long have you lived here, Shana?" Cassidy asked.

"Since I was seven."

Huh. I'd never seen Shana Fitz in our neighborhood before, but I never met any of the kids who went to private schools anyhow.

A blast of icy-cool air met us inside the Fitzes' front door. "Oh, that feels soooo good," Cassidy breathed. "*Air-conditioning.* You're so lucky, Shana. It's so *hot* at my house."

At mine, too. We only had window air conditioners in the bedrooms and just ran them at night, to save pennies and the planet.

Mr. Fitz came barreling down the hallway and Shana introduced us to him. He looked like a big hairy gorilla in purple shorts. Half of his face was painted purple too. "Go, Vikes, eh, girls?" Mr. Fitz boomed. "I took the day off work to go cheer them on at training camp."

"Football season again." Shana blew a raspberry. "Dad's foaming at the mouth. Ignore him. C'mon." She led us into the kitchen, grabbed three Cokes from the refrigerator, then took us upstairs to her room. We stepped inside and Cassidy went, *"Holy cow!"*

"I made Dad paint my room bright yellow," Shana said, "when I found out yellow is Milo's favorite."

Whoa. Another Milo Lennox shrine. Her walls were covered with nearly as many posters as Cassidy's room. I had to hurry up and buy a bunch for my room too!

Cassidy spied some pictures of sports cars and said excitedly, "Porsche 911 Turbos! That's what Milo drives!" Then she leaped over to the big-screen TV in the corner of Shana's bedroom. Sheesh.

"That's my dad's old TV," Shana said. "He's so hooked on sports, he had to have a bigger screen for watching his games on. But this one's good enough for my room."

"Good enough?" Cassidy gasped. "It's fantabulous!" Cassidy ran her fingers over the blank screen. Then she started to drool over Gadget Girl's stacks of videos, CDs and DVDs.

I scratched my cheek hard. Shana's techie-rich dream bedroom made me super-uncomfortable. Annie and I didn't have any of this stuff at our houses. Oh, why did Annie have to move to France? Suddenly I missed her desperately. Two little pools of tears were starting to bubble up behind my eyes . . . when I spied something familiar and comforting on Shana's nightstand. A novel.

Maybe Shana Fitz and I had something in common after all.

I grabbed the book and said, "I haven't read this one, Shana. Is it good?"

Shana rolled her eyes. "That isn't *mine*. My cousin left it here last weekend. Hard-core bookworms like her just bore me so much. 'Oh, have you read *So and So,*' " she said in a super-fake voice. " 'I polished off a book *this thick* in one sitting, blah blah blah.' I want to die from boredom every time girls like that open their yaps."

I shut mine tight.

Shana eyed me suspiciously. Uh-oh. Was she catching on to my true identity? I quickly dropped the book onto the nightstand like it was a poison-dart frog or something. I wiped my fingers on my bibs and thought with a grimace, I can never invite Shana Fitz to my house. There are heaps of books in every room!

Shana hopped over to her cavernous closet and changed into an orange mini. Aaarggh. It was just like Cassidy's! Then Shana said, "Cute band alert," and punched the VCR's Play button.

Cassidy plopped down on the floor, inches from the gargantuan screen, and started to hyperventilate like crazy. She made whiny noises and goo-goo eyes at Milo. "It's like he's looking right into my eyeballs. I *love* him," she said, and swooned, her hand over her mouth.

She was melting like a Popsicle over the pop star. I just did not get what the fuss was all about. Yeah, Milo could play a guitar. But could he build a battery-operated nose-hair clipper, made entirely out of salvaged recyclable junk, the way Greg Twitchell had the year before for the school science fair? Now, *that* was impressive.

I sat down on Shana's hot-pink inflatable chair and began to squirm. Seeing Cassidy so excited over the taped concert made me wonder, would she even want to spend a single minute at my house ever again? The plastic went squeak squeak squeak. I hoped it wouldn't pop on me.

The pounding percussion and screeching guitars blasting out of the TV made my ears throb. Then Shana did something unbelievable. She turned her radio on too, and she turned the volume up even higher than the TV!

"THE KDQB DEEJAY SAID TO STAY TUNED NIGHT AND DAY FOR UPCOMING NEWS OF MILO'S TOUR! IF MILO DOESN'T COME TO THE TWIN CITIES, I'LL DIE! IF HE DOES, I'LL DIE!" Shana yelled over the two competing rock songs.

Ouch! Talk about mega-earache. I'd be deaf before I was twelve! I was *so* close to making the extremely uncool and geeky move of sticking my fingers in my ears when suddenly Shana shrieked, "Cassidy! Turn off the TV. Quick!"

Cassidy jumped up and clicked off the TV. Shana cranked the radio.

The KDQB deejay shouted over the airwaves, *"I'm holding the press release in my hands, girls. Are you ready for this? Milo Lennox is coming to the Twin Cities on tour."*

Cassidy and Shana leaped to their feet and started to scream at the top of their lungs.

4

Secure Your Oxygen Masks

"That's right, girls," the deejay's voice blasted out of Shana's radio. *"Secure your oxygen masks. The Milo Lennox Band just added the Twin Cities to its whirlwind* School Glue *tour. The venue is Woodland Arena. Sunday, September twenty-second, seven o'clock P.M. Call the Woodland Arena box office or TicketKing for more information now!"*

Shana and Cassidy jumped onto Shana's bed and bounced up and down, yelping and hollering and shrieking.

"Can you *believe* it?" Cassidy screamed. "I can't *wait* to see that super-hot celeb!"

"I get to see my favorite crush *live*!" Shana hollered. "Milo *rules*!"

Hmm, Milo was cute, but Greg was definitely cuter, if you asked me. Well, at least pretend like you care, Cathy, I mean Cat, I told myself. "Oh wow, dyn-o-mite, Milo's coming to town," I murmured, and waved my arms limply.

Shana stopped flying around and put her hands on her hips. "Do you even *like* the Milo Lennox Band, Cat?" she demanded over the blaring radio.

Oops. My thespian skills needed polishing. I had to be more convincing here.

"Are you kidding, I *love* that hottie Milo Lennox!" I screeched. Like a thunderbolt, I leaped onto Shana's bed. I began to bounce with all the muscle power my long skinny legs could muster. Then I launched into the best screaming fan impression I could produce. I screamed with full lung power for practically a whole minute, thinking, Now, *this* should convince them I'm bonkers for Milo!

Cassidy nodded knowingly. "That is *so* how I feel about him too, Cat!"

But Shana's eyes got as narrow as guitar strings. She was not buying my act. She pointed a finger in my face and said, "Your crazy yelling is totally phony. You don't even like the Milo Lennox Band, do you?"

I gulped and started to babble in quivery self-defense, "That's not true! Totally not! Uh, I mean, I understand Milo's appeal on a logical level. . . . He's, um, physically appealing to a degree and all that. . . . And, uh, I've noticed a pleasant mix of harmony and melody in his songs with an occasional interesting dissonant note—"

Shana gave a big blasting snort. "What language are you speaking?" she shrieked, slapping her bare leg. "You sound like an *encyclopedia*!"

Oops. Massive mistake here. This aggressive girl made me so nervous, I'd completely forgotten to check my vocabulary at the door!

Cassidy stared at me. She looked surprised and confused. Oh no. Now she thought I was a geekgirl too!

"Uh—I was only doing my professor impersonation," I stammered. "It was, er, a joke!"

Cassidy's confused look disappeared. "I knew it, Cat—you're so funny!" She laughed loudly.

I sighed with relief. At least Cassidy bought my fib, but Shana still looked totally unconvinced. Then she hopped off her bed and left the room. Oh, great. I'd literally grossed her out the door. She couldn't even stand to be in the same room with me!

Half a minute later, Shana came back with the Minneapolis yellow pages and a cordless telephone. Phew. She just had to make a phone call.

"I've got to order tickets this second," she said. "Front-row seats, of course. I'll charge Dad's and my tickets on his card. He always lets me. He'll take us to the concert, too."

Who's "us"? I wondered.

Shana handed Cassidy the phone. "I'll look up the number. You dial," she said bossily.

"My puh-leasure," Cassidy said with a happy grin,

apparently not bothered a bit at being ordered around. "Milo, you cutie . . . here we come!"

Shana opened the yellow pages to "stadiums" and was reaching to turn down the radio when suddenly the deejay came back on the airwaves, hollering at top volume, *"Another news flash from the Milo Lennox Band, just handed to me here in the studio, girls. There's a preconcert dance contest at five P.M., September twenty-second, in the Woodland Arena parking lot. That's two hours before the concert begins, girls. The winner gets to be a backup dancer* onstage *with Milo, Duke and Jarvis for that night's show. Practice those moves, girls!"*

Shana's jaw dropped so far it was practically hanging on her shag carpet. She didn't move for about ten seconds; then she gasped and started to bop all over her bedroom, shrieking, "I'm going to win that contest! I'm going to win, win, *win*! I get to be a backup dancer for Milo Lennox!" Her long brown hair flew all over the place. She clutched her heart and looked like she was going to die.

I raised my eyebrows. *Now* who was the crazy one here, huh?

Shana bopped over and grabbed the telephone book. "We've got to get front-row seats," she murmured, scanning the yellow pages. "And I'm going to be first in line for that dance audition." She looked hard at Cassidy. "You're not trying out too, are you?"

"No!" Cassidy giggled. "I want to watch the concert, not be in it. Besides, you know all the dance steps to Milo's songs. You'll win for sure. I want *you* to!"

Shana grinned and said, "Goody."

She didn't ask me if I planned to audition. Was that such a ludicrous idea?

Cassidy breathed, "Oh, I can't believe I get to see Milo up close and personal. Look at me, I'm shaking like Jell-O."

Shana read the number out loud while Cassidy dialed with a spastic pointer finger.

"The bone is fizzy." Cassidy giggled. "Oops, I mean, the phone is busy. I always mix up words when I'm nervous or excited. You call, Shana."

Shana grabbed the phone, dialed fast and blurted to the operator, "How much are Milo Lennox Band tickets? I want a front-row seat and so does my friend Cassidy. Can I put mine on my dad's charge card right now? . . . Oh . . . cheap bleacher seats are forty-five dollars . . . uh-huh . . . and front-row seats are one hundred dollars each . . . okay . . . thanks."

A *hundred* bucks? For *one* ticket?

That was a relief! I was sure Cassidy wouldn't blow *all* her savings on one overly inflated ticket. Good. Then Shana could go alone with her big hairy date—her dad.

"Oh, we *have* to get front-row seats!" Cassidy squealed. "Should I run home and get my money right now, Shana?"

My mouth fell open. I leaned over and whispered, "But Cassidy, that's so much money!"

Cassidy looked at me sweetly and replied, "Cat, I'd spend a *thousand* dollars to see Milo in concert if I had that much money!"

I gnawed another fingernail down to a nub.

Shana clicked off the phone and rattled on, "Don't get

your money yet, Cassidy. The lady at the box office said the tickets go on sale at TicketKing next Friday morning at six A.M. sharp. That's September sixth. We'll be first in line. We have to be, to get front-row seats. We can spend the night in the parking lot in my dad's car."

"Terrif!" Cassidy said.

"I know my dad won't mind," Shana added. "Just don't forget your sleeping bag and your hundred bucks, Cassidy."

Who was I, Invisible Girl? I started to speak and then I realized the next Thursday was a school night. My mom would never let me go!

Shana looked at me. "What?" she demanded. "Why are you all bug-eyed?"

"That's a school night," I peeped.

"So?" she said snottily. Boy, this girl needed to carry around whole boxes of tissues to wipe away her snotty remarks. "My parents don't care. Besides, I've done it before. My dad and I camped out to get Juicy Melon Band and Reform Skool tickets."

"Oh," I squeaked. I looked at Cassidy and asked quietly, "Will your mom let you?"

Cassidy nodded and grinned. "My mom says Milo Lennox is a turtledove who sings like a lark. How about you, Cat? Can you come?"

Oh, Cassidy was *so* nice. I wanted her for a friend so much. But Miss Moneybags Fitz with her cable hookup was drawing Cassidy away from me like a high-powered magnet.

"Well?" Shana said impatiently. "Are you coming or not?"

Somehow, some way, I had to keep up with Shana. I couldn't stay home on September twenty-second. How uncool would that look to Cassidy? I *had* to go to Milo's *School Glue* tour concert; otherwise Cassidy and Shana would bond like glue and I'd be the odd girl out!

I took a deep breath and announced, "I'm going with you to Milo's concert. But my mom might not let me sleep out next week. If she doesn't, will you take my money and buy a ticket for me, Cassidy? A front-row one so I can sit next to you?"

"Of course," Cassidy replied kindly, and beamed at me.

"Thanks!" I headed for Shana's door and mumbled, "Bye, Shana."

"Wait, Cat," Cassidy said. "Do you want to go to Resurrection Duds now?"

It was super-nice of her to remember. But I replied, "No, Cassidy. I can't spend any money on clothes now. My fifteen dollars has to go toward a concert ticket. If I add five from next week's allowance, I'll only have twenty. I still have to come up with eighty more dollars before next Thursday."

Shana looked at me sideways and muttered, "What are you, a human calculator?"

My face grew warm. "Bye," I said. "I need to start earning big bucks right away."

"Good luck, Cat!" Cassidy said. "I hope you can come to the concert!"

"Me too." I smiled at Cassidy. Then I flashed a totally fake

✳ **43** ✳

grin at Shana, gave a determined toss of my lopsided ponytail and marched out her bedroom door.

I ran all the way home and found Dad in the living room. His head was stuffed up the chimney; he was trying to fix something before the cold September air blew in from Canada.

"Hey, Dad?" I said. "Do you maybe, just perhaps, have a little bundle of cash stashed under a mattress somewhere? Or taped under a drawer?"

No response. I tapped his back and yelled, "Listen, Dad! If you let me borrow a little of your nest egg—like about eighty bucks' worth—I promise, I'll never ask for anything ever again, as long as I live. Even if I live to be a hundred and twenty!"

Dad pulled his sooty bald head out of the chimney and laughed. Hard. His eyes started to squirt H_2O like a couple of leaky faucets.

Oh, brother. All right then, I thought with a jerk of my chin, I'll try my sister.

I knew Lizzie had a bloated piggy bank. She was saving for her very own set of *Encyclopaedia Britannica*. I dashed upstairs to her room and asked if I could borrow a substantial chunk of her life savings.

Lizzie laughed. "That's funny," she said, "nobody has ever mistaken me for a cute little personal ATM before."

Sheesh. I marched down the hall and called my grandma Victoria on the phone.

"Grandma!" I said. "Hi! Say, is there any chance I could possibly get . . . a four-year advance on my Christmas money gifts? I really need a nice big pile of cold hard cash right this minute."

Grandma Victoria burst out laughing. "Oh, Catherine! *Thank* you for calling. My goodness, I needed a good laugh today. Ha ha ha ha ha—"

"You're welcome, Grandma. See you soon. Bye." I hung up the phone and groaned. Three strikes. Was I out? Not yet.

I grabbed the phone again and called Mom at the high school.

"Mom," I said, "there's this Milo Lennox Band concert on September twenty-second—"

"Who in the world is Marvin Xerox?"

"*Milo Lennox,* Mom. Cassidy is going to his concert and I want to go too. All I need is a little help from Mr. Visa."

Mom laughed. "I cut up the card, Cat. No Visa until Dad's back on full salary."

"So get American Express," I insisted.

Mom let out a big guffaw. "If you want to go to that concert, you'll have to use your own allowance, Cath—I mean Cat. You know we're on a very tight budget this year. And the new toilet we bought in June sucked up our savings, so to speak."

"But my puny allowance wouldn't begin to buy a Milo Lennox Band concert ticket." I sighed.

"Why not?" Mom asked cluelessly. "How much is a ticket?"

I played with the telephone cord for a couple of seconds, then peeped, "Um, a hundred dollars per seat."

"A hundred dollars!" Mom screeched. "For *one* ticket?"

Ouch! I held the receiver away from my throbbing ear-drum. Mom calmed down, then said, "That's ridiculous. Out of the question."

"Mom," I protested, "Cassidy gets to go. And Shana is going."

"Shana who?"

"Fitz. She's a new sixth grader I met at our school today. I *have* to go to that concert with those guys, Mom."

"Well," Mom said, sighing, "you'll need to try to earn the money, then. Say, how about baby-sitting again?"

"Again?" I said, my eyes popping wide open. "How about never? You know I can't stand grubby little fingers and poopy Pampers."

Mom laughed and said, "Well, Cat, you'll have to learn to tolerate them if you want to get to that Melvin Mailbox con-cert. Is he a classical guitarist? Or does he sing?"

"Um, he sings, Mom," I mumbled. "Pop music."

"What's that, honey? I didn't hear you."

I took a deep breath, then repeated the words loudly into the phone: "Pop music, Mom!"

Mom was quiet for a weird long moment. Then she said, "But that kind of music gives me hives, darling—"

"You wouldn't have to hear a single note of it," I said firmly. "Not even a half note or a quarter note. I'm the one go-ing to his concert."

"We'll see," Mom said; then she had to dash off to a meeting.

I huffed, hung up and marched upstairs to check my e-mail. My box came up empty—again! Cripes. Was Paris a black hole or had Annie traveled there by way of the Bermuda Triangle?

Well, I had to send her my news du jour anyhow. My single typing finger flew across the keyboard. I pecked:

I know I've stuffed your mailbox already, but a ton of crazy stuff has happened here since just yesterday, Annie! I met a really nice girl named Cassidy. Do you remember her from last year? She invited me to a concert. Can you believe it? Milo Lennox—he's all over Sizzle Pop. I've got a massive money-crunch problem, though! The tickets cost $100. If you have any brainy moneymaking ideas, send them ASAP. But I need your girl genius mostly for this: there's another new kid at our school named Shana. I just know she's going to try to steal Cassidy away from me. How can I stop her? Puh-leeeeez write soon! Luv, Cat.
P.S. That's my cool new nickname. What do you think?

I pushed the Send button and smiled. Annie would know what to do. She was always an Idea Machine, churning out great solutions.

I logged off, then hopped over to Dad's desk. I grabbed his old transistor radio and spent twenty whole minutes trying to find KDQB.

I surfed FM from beginning to end, then AM. No luck.

Back on the FM dial, way down by 90, I finally found KDQB. I turned the volume on low and leaned back in Dad's study chair to listen for a Milo Lennox tune. I had to learn his songs by heart so I could sing along with Cassidy!

A few minutes later, Dad stuck his head in the study door and asked, "Have you seen my reading glasses, Cat?"

That very second, "Goddess Caffeina" came on the air! Triple-quick, I cranked the radio full blast so I could hear every word. Dad jumped about two feet.

I grabbed a pen and notepad and started to write down the lyrics super-fast.

"Turn that racket down, Cat!" Dad hollered.

"Just a second!" I waved my left arm to shush Dad up while I scribbled furiously with my right.

The song ended and I slapped down my pen. "Got it!" I turned the radio off and grinned happily at Dad.

He was gawking at me like I'd sprouted a radio tower out the top of my head. "That's not music," he said, and grimaced. "That's noise pollution!"

I laughed and said, "Maybe, Dad. But whatever it is, I need to memorize it right now." I put my nose to the notepad and got busy. One etched-in-the-head Milo song was a darn good start toward fitting in with Cassidy and Shana.

5

Whoa There, Buckaroos

"Aaaarggh." I groaned and stuck my head under my pillow.

It was Tuesday morning. The second I woke up I remembered what I had to do. But closing my eyes again couldn't keep the pictures out of my mind: boogery noses . . . ear-piercing tantrums . . .

Okay. So I had an attitude about launching a baby-sitting career. Blame it on the one time I tried it, the summer before, when I was ten.

The little brat's name was Lucy. She was four years old. I accidentally touched one of her Barbies and she went totally ballistic on me. Her sharp little fangs locked on to my wrist and drew a decent snack for Dracula.

My nerve endings were fractured. I vowed never to be a parent. If I ever did have a kid, we'd just skip the fourth year. We'd move right from age three to five.

The very idea of kiddie care gave me the willies, like the time I bit into a big strawberry and a huge worm was inside. I hadn't eaten any of the worm, but knowing how close I had come to nibbling on it made me shiver for a full hour afterward.

My willies this morning weren't as far up the shudder-o-meter, but still, eeewww. Anyhow, shivers aside, I *had* to get to that concert!

"This amount of desperation," I told myself firmly, rolling out of bed, "calls for desperate measures. It's time to bite the bullet and . . . baby-sit."

Besides, it was just about my only hope for employment (considering child labor laws).

I pulled on my old baby bib overalls and muttered, "I'll fit right in with the diaper set wearing these things." I tugged on my old tennies and trudged downstairs. It was time to pound the pavement and line up some baby-sitting jobs. I'd kindly ask the kiddies' mommies or daddies to give me sixteen baby-sitting hours. Sixteen times five bucks per hour. That'd equal eighty bucks for one well-earned Milo Lennox Band concert ticket.

Lizzie was lying on the living room floor, her little freckled nose stuck in our giant *National Geographic* atlas. "Has Mom left for work already?" I asked.

"Uh-huh."

"Where's Dad?"

"Basement. Fixing the broken rocking chair."

"Tell him I'm going to go earn eighty bucks, okay? I'll be back soon." I grabbed a granola bar for breakfast, tugged on one of Dad's old fishing hats to cover my bed head (I'd finally dismantled the ponytail the night before), then marched up the street.

There weren't any kids on our block who I'd exactly call a nanny's dream, so I turned the corner and spied a kiddie tricycle in front of 518 Radner Lane. This family was new. I remembered seeing a moving van there back in June.

I stepped up to the front door. Slam, slam, slam. I gave the lion knocker a few hard whacks. The door flew open. A lady with wild hair and wild eyes stood in the doorway, a plastic basket full of laundry in her arms.

I remembered seeing her at QuikPick one day chasing after some runaway apples and oranges that a kid had knocked off the fruit display. Surely her sweet baby hadn't done that. Probably a bratty nephew visiting from Wisconsin or somewhere.

"Yes?"

"Hi-my-name-is-Cat-Carlson-I-live-around-the-corner-I'm-looking-for-baby-sitting-jobs-and—"

The lady's eyes started to spin. "A baby-sitter," she breathed. "And I know you. I mean, I know your mother. Elsa Carlson, right?"

I nodded eagerly.

"I met your mother at the block party in July. I am *so* pleased to meet you, too, Cat. I'm Mrs. Harris." Suddenly Mrs. H's face crumpled up and her eyes got all misty. She grabbed a fistful of my T-shirt and hauled me into her house. "You're like an angel on my doorstep. Throw your hat any old place, Cat." She took off my fishing cap and chucked it on a chair. I felt my bed head go sproing. Oh, well. I sure didn't need to impress the baby.

"My in-laws just called and invited themselves to dinner," Mrs. H rattled on, leading me through the living room, ". . . my husband won't be home from work until six-thirty tonight. . . . There isn't a scrap of food in the fridge that isn't moldy. . . . This place is a disaster. . . . The boys woke up at five A.M. today and I know they'll refuse to nap this afternoon. . . ."

The "boys"? What was this plural stuff? There was more than one baby?

Mrs. H grabbed her purse and keys. "Have you baby-sat before, Cat?" she asked.

"Oh, on multiple occasions," I lied. "I seize and adore every child-care opportunity that comes my way."

"That is just wonderful," Mrs. H said, clapping her hand to her heart. "Well, let's introduce you to the boys, then I'll dash to the dry cleaner, the post office and the market. The errands will go ten times faster by myself."

She led me into the den.

Two massive preschoolers stood with their chubby faces

frozen six inches in front of a blaring TV screen. One had his finger stuck up his nose. The other had his hand down his pants. Eek. These weren't babies. They were mini–grown-ups!

The roly-poly boys were held spellbound by Wile E. Coyote trying to commit Road Runnericide. Mrs. H stepped in front of the TV, bent down to runny-nose level and said, "Boys? Turn around and say hello to Cat."

The tubby twins whined and tried to shove their mother aside. She was totally blocking their view of the tube.

"Say hello to Cat *now,*" Mrs. H growled through a smile.

The boys turned clockwise a fraction of an inch and mumbled, "Hi."

In that instant, I realized that these two squirts looked exactly alike. They were twins! And uh-oh. I recognized them from the neighborhood block party. These two wrigglers had knocked over the dessert table and gotten totally covered in cake. What had I gotten myself into?

Before I could back out, Mrs. H thanked me from the depths of her heart, flew to the door, locked it behind her and zoomed off in her SUV.

The twins moved even closer to the blaring television.

"Hello," I said cautiously.

No response. Hmm. Maybe if I left the TV on, this kiddie-care thing wouldn't be so tough. . . .

I flopped onto the couch and peeked at my watch. Only fifteen hours and fifty-seven minutes to go. Then buh-bye to all baby-sitting jobs for the rest of my life!

Suddenly the cartoon ended, a commercial came on and the tube lost its magnetic hold on their boogery little noses. The rotund twosome turned around and leaped onto me. One landed on my legs, the other on my shoulders.

"I wanna wrestle!"

"I'm the Masked Marvel."

"No, *I* am."

They were jumping all over me, practically tearing my limbs off and my hair out. "Whoa there, buckaroos," I growled in my best commando voice. I peeled them off me and held them tightly by the wrists. "What are your names?"

"Quentin."

"Quincy."

My eyebrows shot up. *"Really,"* I said. "And what's your mommy's name, Quentina?" I laughed.

Four blue eyes stared at me blankly.

"Okay. Um. How old are you guys?"

"Four."

"Four."

Oh no. Two four-year-olds. In the same house. For *sixteen* hours. I gulped and stepped back.

"I have to poop," said Quentin.

"You're kidding," I said.

Quentin ran to the bathroom. Quincy chased after him. I followed them lamely, then stood in the hallway, wringing my fingers, for a full three minutes. "Do you need any help with, uh, anything in there?" I called.

"I need help wiping," yelled Quentin.

Eewww. Gross! Was this in my job description?

"And Quincy has pee all over him."

"What?" I squawked. I darted into the bathroom and saw a big yellow puddle on the white tile floor. Quentin sat perched on the pot. Quincy stood facing the throne. His Winnie the Pooh jumpsuit was soaked from collar to ankles.

"What in the world happened?" I asked.

"I forgot to push my wee wee down and Quincy was in the way of my pee pee."

"Oh," I said weakly. "Okay. Um, does your mommy have any rubber gloves?"

Identical blank stares had *duh* written all over them.

Soooo, using the tip-most tips of two fingers, I peeled Quincy's clothes off. Then I discovered that Quentin's sweatpants and underpants were soaked too.

I breathed through my mouth exclusively, trying not to take in even the tiniest whiff. Suddenly my gag mechanism kicked into high gear. "My gosh," I muttered, trying superhard not to hurl, "what a girl has to go through to get a Milo ticket."

The second I stripped Q & Q, they tore out of the bathroom, buck naked and giggling hysterically.

"Wait, Quentin!" I called. "We have to wipe your bottom. Don't sit on the white couch!" I chased after him with a wad of t.p.

I couldn't get a fingerhold on either of the squirmy worms. How was I going to get *two* of them washed up and dressed?

I tore after them, through every room in that big house, trying to lasso those little giggling buckaroos. They wriggled under beds, where I couldn't reach them, their pudgy nudie butts jiggling like white pudding.

We made a second lap through the house. I was charging through the front hallway after those naked little numbskulls when suddenly the lock turned in the front door.

Mrs. Harris stuck her head inside and called in a singsong voice, "Oh, Cat! It's just me! I forgot my checkbook!"

The two bare-bottom Q-balls rolled around on the front hallway rug, laughing like banshees.

Mrs. H's smile disappeared. Wide-eyed, she squeaked, "Why are you two boys prancing about in your *birthday suits*?"

I grimaced and tried to explain everything.

Mrs. H dropped her purse on the floor. "I suppose you need more experience before you can handle twins, Cat," she said, her shoulders all droopy. Boy, she looked tired.

"I'm so sorry, Mrs. Harris."

"That's all right, Cat." She sighed. "Maybe when you're a couple years older, we'll try again."

I stuck Dad's old fishing hat back on my bed head and nearly croaked as I uttered the words, "And you don't, um, have to pay me for these fifteen minutes of baby-sitting, either."

Then I slunk to the door and dragged my holey tennies on home.

I flopped down on the couch in our hot living room and

wondered, How will I ever earn that pile of cold hard cash now? Suddenly I sat upright. Raking! I'd rake sixteen yards at five bucks per yard. I'd do it all week, earning a front-row concert ticket the robust way. Yesss!

I hopped off the couch and ran to the window.

There was only one problem. Not one leaf on our entire street had fallen to the ground yet. That wouldn't happen for a few more weeks.

Hmmm. I needed a quick solution to this cash-flow dilemma. I decided to try meditation.

I hopped back on the couch and tried to get comfortable in the lotus position. I pressed my fingers to my temples and chanted, "Money. Money. Money."

Within a minute a fuzzy vision floated across my gray matter and slowly . . . came into . . . focus. . . .

I saw Cassidy . . . and Shana. They were . . . swimming, together . . . just the two of them . . .

. . . giggling and splashing about . . . in a pool of . . .

. . . refreshing cool green cash.

6

Cat's Dog-Walking Service

"**H**i! Please leave a machine on our answering message at the beep. Thanks!"

I barely noticed Cassidy's mistake. Why wasn't she answering the phone? It was only ten o'clock Tuesday morning. I'd just gotten back from baby-sitting. Oh no . . . was Cassidy at Shana's house already?

Double drat! I should've called her first thing that day, before Shana had a chance to make plans with her!

My heart started to beat fast as I left a message on the tape. "Hi, Cassidy, it's me, Cat. I wondered if you wanted to help me make business cards and put them in mailboxes. I just got a new idea for how to earn money for a concert ticket. I'm going to start a dog-walking service—"

"Hey. Who's this?" The machine clicked off and a guy's voice came on the line.

"This is Cat. Who's this?"

"Baird. Cassidy took her swimsuit to Shana's. They're going to Como Pool."

"But the pool doesn't open till one! Do you think they'll hang out at Shana's until then?"

"Beats me. I'm not Cassidy's social secretary." Baird yawned, mumbled "Bye" and hung up.

I dropped the phone and paced the kitchen floor like a caged tigress. Cassidy had called me a *friend* on Monday. But today, she was totally leaving me out of her plans! Cripes, I'd never felt this left out in my life. But then, I'd always had Annie.

I swallowed hard, then got busy making a couple dozen business cards to distract myself.

This is what they looked like:

```
CAT'S DOG-WALKING SERVICE
YOUR DOG'S IN GOOD PAWS WITH CAT.
A BOW-WOW BARGAIN!
ONLY ONE PUNY BUCK PER LONG POOCH WALK!
CALL CAT TODAY! 655-4959
```

Then I grabbed the pile, shouted "Bye" to my dad and started passing them out to neighbors.

Ten houses later, I had my first job! It was for Dietrich, a retired German professor who knew my dad. He had a giant sheepdog he was too busy to walk that day. Wolfgang was a haystack of white and gray hair. I couldn't see his eyes at all, just like Greg.

Dietrich handed me Wolfgang's leash and a large plastic bag. "To clean up zeh *big* mess," Dietrich said. "Volfgang only understands German. Do you speak German, *Liebchen*?"

"I'm afraid not, sir," I replied, "but I do know a little Latin. For example, a sentence my dad taught me is 'Move your *gluteus maximus* off the couch and *carpe diem*!' " (Translation: "Get your duff off that sofa and make the most of this day!")

"Oh, vell. Maybe just a short walk then, *Liebchen,* since you might have trouble," said Dietrich. "Good luck. You vill need it. Bye-bye!"

Wolfgang tore off down Lucille Street Hill, tugging me along behind him. Boy, he was strong, like Hercules on four legs! Holding on to that leash with every bit of gripping power in my ten digits, I got dragged past my house, over two blocks and up another three. Suddenly Wolfgang stopped for a bathroom break right on Greg Twitchell's perfectly manicured front lawn!

My face caught fire as Wolfgang took a number two of anaconda proportions. Blushing furiously and hoping like mad Greg wasn't looking out the window, I whispered, "Hurry up!"

Finally, Wolfgang finished. I bent over to pick up the mess with the plastic bag and just then Greg's front door opened. I glanced over and nearly croaked.

"Hi!" Greg called with a grin.

My face an inferno, I scooped the python-sized poo into the big Baggie—just as Greg came loping toward me. I chucked the heavy bag over my shoulder and it sailed skyward—and landed on the Twitchells' garage roof. Oops.

Thankfully, Greg didn't notice. "An Old English sheepdog!" he exclaimed, and gave Wolfgang a bunch of hearty pats on the head. "For some reason I identify with this breed."

Maybe it's your identical haircuts, I thought, and smiled.

Greg swatted playfully at Wolfgang's front legs. "You just want to romp all day, don't you, boy?"

Wolfgang went "WOOF!" and ran in a circle around Greg. The long leash wrapped around Greg's skinny ankles . . . and mine, too.

"Wolfgang, stop it," I demanded.

But Greg had the huge dog all revved up now. Wolfgang ran circles around us, pulling the leather strap tighter around our legs. It quickly drew Greg and me closer—until we were like two sardines in a tin. My left shoulder, arm and hip were smashed against Greg's. Suddenly we lost our balance and toppled backward, our rear ends landing on the grass with a thud.

Then Wolfgang ran out of leash. He sat down on his haunches beside me, squished against my right shoulder. The three of us sat there, tethered tightly together, unmoving.

I was sandwiched between two sheepdogs. Nose to nose, Greg and I wiggled and jiggled, but we couldn't loosen that leather snare a millimeter.

Boy, I was glad I'd brushed my teeth that morning. I just wished Wolfgang had. P.U. He was panting hard and slobbering all over me.

But I was even more uncomfortable sitting so close to Greg. I was glad his woolly mane covered his sapphire peepers. A view of those gems so close could make a girl faint.

"Wolfgang, get up. Move back," I ordered. He refused to budge. He was all tired out. "Oh, that's right, Wolfgang only understands German!"

"Volfgang," Greg said sternly, *"Steh auf! Geh links!"*

Immediately, Wolfgang got up off his haunches and lumbered counterclockwise. Then Greg kept saying, *"Noch einmal!"*

Like a huge, hairy remote-control toy, Wolfgang obeyed Greg's commands. Soon we were completely freed of that leash.

I stepped back from Greg and stared at him in amazement. "Where did you learn to speak German?" I asked in shock.

"Oh, I pick up languages here and there," he replied with a humble shrug.

I gawked at him, totally impressed. This boy was full of surprises!

✳ ✳ ✳

At one o'clock, Dad drove Lizzie and me to Como Pool. I asked him to take us, and I knew he couldn't say no for budget reasons—our family swimming pass hadn't expired yet.

I simply had to try to slip into Cassidy and Shana's poolside party, even if I wasn't invited. Maybe Cassidy had just forgotten to call me up. (I sure hoped so!)

Cassidy spied me right away when I stepped inside the pool gate. She and Shana lay on towels at the far end of the deck. "Cat! Hi!" she cried in surprise. "Come over here!"

Oh, this was fabulous! She seemed *happy* to see me! "Just a second!" I shouted. Lizzie and I ducked into the women's locker room and tugged on our old faded suits.

"Now, Lizzie," I said firmly, "don't ask Cassidy or Shana to quiz you on world capitals or anything like that, okay?"

Lizzie laughed. "What are you talking about, Cat? We need to test each other on all those CPR and mouth-to-mouth resuscitation steps when we're at the *pool,* for Pete's sakes."

"Lizzie, don't you dare—"

But she ran off to the diving board and didn't hear me. I slunk over to Cassidy and Shana and realized at once that I should have stayed home . . . because they were wearing nearly identical super-cute striped bikinis, the color of rainbow sherbet.

Shana took off her sunglasses and looked me up and down. "Nice suit," she sneered.

Nice mouth, I thought, grinding my jawbones. But I didn't dare say that out loud. Talking back to Shana would not earn me a pass into this clique.

I glanced down and studied my old one-piece. Okay. So it was covered with nubbies, from sitting on cement pool decks at lessons. And it had a saggy baggy stretched-out butt, from too many cartwheels in the yard under the sprinkler. And it was droopy in my voluptuous (not) chest region, due to the fact that I had Chihuahua-sized buds at best. All right, so maybe I could use a new suit, I admitted silently.

But who appointed Miss Fitz fashion cop anyhow?

I sure wouldn't mind some backup, I thought, nibbling a fingernail. I guessed Cassidy hadn't heard because she was super-busy now, scribbling in a notebook. "I'm designing Shana's audition outfit, Cat," she mumbled, drawing furiously. "It's going to be covered with rhinestones, using my glue gun. She'll be a star!"

"Oh." I quickly slipped into the water and stayed submerged from the shoulders down. I managed to keep my suit safely hidden from Shana but couldn't get a word in edgewise. I treaded water just two feet from their towels for nearly two hours, but it was like they were in one bubble and I was in another. They jabbered on and on about their designs for the audition outfit. Then they blabbered on and on about the I LOVE YOU, MILO signs they planned to carry at the concert.

"I can make those signs for you guys, if you want," I offered. "I'm good at making signs—" Just then a little kid dunked me and I came up spluttering.

I sighed and gave up.

I kept my ugly suit under H_2O cover until Dad returned to pick Lizzie and me up at three-thirty. But I'd forgotten to put on sunscreen and got fried from the collarbone up.

At four-thirty I logged on to the Internet and the speakers droned in computerese, *"You've got mail."*

Finally! In a flash, I opened my box. Yesss! A letter from Annie! I devoured the screen eagerly:

Bonjour, CATHY (I prefer that to Cat actually):
At last we found an electrical cord that works with these European outlets. I enjoyed your first seventeen e-mails, but imagine my shock at the eighteenth. Do you have pop bubbles in the think tank? A pop concert? For one thing, those songs don't even make any sense. Secondly, $300 could buy a 3-year subscription to Newsweek. Or 500 pounds of dog food for all the hungry strays at the humane society. Here's a helpful idea, since you asked: let Shana have Cassidy. Why would you want to hang out with girls like that in the first place? Au revoir, Annie

I gawked at the screen. I could practically hear Annie call me Shallow Girl! She'd never said a mean word to me before, not *once* in eleven years!

I'd thought Annie would understand.

The sprinkler system in my eyes kicked in. Wiping my tears away, I logged off triple-quick. No way would I respond to that note, not tonight. Maybe not tomorrow, either . . .

I dragged my bare feet to my bedroom, turned my air conditioner on low and crawled into bed. A big lump of loneliness lay at the bottom of my stomach. Suddenly I wasn't sure I had a single true friend on either side of the Atlantic.

✳ ✳ ✳

Wednesday morning, I waited for Cassidy to call me first, for a change.

She didn't. I knew I'd feel less lonely if I could at least e-mail Annie. But we weren't speaking, or "E-ing," I should say.

At five o'clock, I got a job walking a bulldog named Norbert. I walked Norbert an extra-long distance, way above the call of duty, so I could pass by Cassidy's house. I tied Norbert to the McDews' old peeling picket fence, then knocked on their front door.

Mrs. McDew answered the door and gave me a super-warm greeting.

"Cassidy told me all about you, honey! Come on in!" Mrs. McDew was a larger version of Cassidy, with hair as big and a smile as sweet. I stepped inside.

"She thinks you're a real nice girl," Mrs. McDew said all singsongy.

Those words sure made me smile. I hoped they were true. "Can I see her?"

"I'm afraid Cassidy's not home right now, honey." Mrs. McDew slipped off her heels and rubbed her toes. "She left with her overnight bag the minute I got home from work. But not until I got the dozen good-bye kisses I insisted on!"

"Her overnight bag?" I peeped.

"That's right, honey. And her mosquito lotion, sleeping

✳ 66 ✳

bag, hiking boots and a fishing rod she borrowed from Baird. She didn't tell you? She went up to Shana Fitz's big fancy log cabin way up north for the long holiday weekend. She'll be back Sunday afternoon."

My face must've looked as sad as a basset hound's, because Mrs. McDew took my arm and led me into the living room and sat me down on the couch next to Great-granny Rose.

Great-granny Rose looked at me dimly and said, "Hello, Shana, honey. Nice to see you again. You're such a beautiful girl."

"I'm Cat, not Shana," I murmured. Then I stuck a string of hair in my mouth and sucked on it, nursing my misery.

Mrs. McDew looked at me long and hard for a minute. Then she squished in beside me on the little old couch and took my hand. "You feel left out, don'tcha, honey?" she asked quietly.

I nodded.

"Do you know how I know that?" Mrs. McDew asked.

I shook my head.

"Because I've seen that look in Cassidy's eyes for years and years. She's always the new girl in some new town at some new school. It's worse when her daddy's gone on the road. She really gets lonesome for him. Cassidy needs all the friends she can find here in St. Paul, Cat." Mrs. McDew squeezed my fingers and gave me a super-sympathetic look. "I hope you and Cassie can be good friends too."

Mrs. McDew's gaze worked like onions on my own eyes. The saltwater pools behind them began to fill up.

"I hope so too, Mrs. McDew," I said, swallowing hard. If only Shana would allow it.

I was halfway down the driveway when Mrs. McDew came rushing out with a bag. "I just found this on the porch, Cat." She beamed and handed it to me. "It has your name on it. I knew my Cassidy was a sweetheart."

And she was right. Inside was a Walkman, a *School Glue* cassette and a note that said, "Thought these would make your job more fun! I got a Discman for my birthday, so you can borrow these as long as you want. Talk to you more soon!"

✳ ✳ ✳

Friday through Sunday of Labor Day weekend, I labored like mad, walking poodles and terriers and spaniels. I imagined Cassidy and Shana having a blast up north, making s'mores over campfires and waterskiing behind speedboats, while I picked up stinky dog poop in the blistering hot Twin Cities. Still, it was comforting to have Cassidy's Walkman.

During each long pooch outing, I listened to a couple more of Milo's songs. I rolled my eyes at "I'm a Greaseball, She's a Goofball," the fifth song on side one. "So maybe I'm a greaseball," Milo wailed, "but hey, she threw a French fry at me . . . I think that gorgeous goofball loves meeeeee . . ." *Buh-rother.* These lyrics were as deep as a plastic kiddie swimming pool. Maybe Annie was right. I *was* going to a *ton* of trouble earning money to hear music I didn't even like. But I wasn't ready to tell her that yet—or give up.

I kept listening to the songs on side one, in my quest to memorize every Milo word.

Sunday morning, I even offered to walk Puff free of charge. I hugged him and played with him a long time. That made me feel closer to Cassidy when she was out of town.

I earned fifteen dollars walking dogs over the holiday weekend. Including my week's allowance, that made thirty-seven dollars total so far. I had four days left to earn sixty-three bucks.

I needed a financial miracle.

7

Hot Pink Hair

"**S**avers Plus has the best prices," Mom said, and sighed. It was Monday morning, Labor Day, and she was skimming the newspaper ads. My mom hated all forms of shopping (materialism in general gave her a headache), but we couldn't put off buying school supplies any longer. "Okay. Let's go, girls."

"Can Cassidy come along?" I asked. "I'm sure she's back from"—I could hardly spit out the two troublesome words—"Shana's cabin."

"Fine. But this has to be a quick trip, Cat. I still have so much to do before classes begin tomorrow."

"Thanks, Mom. I promise we'll be fast."

I grabbed the kitchen phone and called Cassidy. "Oh,

Cat!" she squealed over the line. "I saw a real live bear in the woods up at Shana's cabin and I was so *scared*!"

I got super-quiet.

Cassidy got quiet at my quietness. "Um, Cat? I'm sorry you couldn't go up north with us. I asked Shana if you could, but she said the Jeep was too small, with all the gear and stuff."

That bumped my Happy Meter up a couple of notches. "Thanks for asking if I could go and for loaning me your Walkman." I swear Cassidy's heart was as big as her hair. "Have you done your school-supply shopping yet?"

"Of course not." She giggled. "I haven't even thought about school."

My Happy Meter took a dip, but I pushed on. "I'm going to Savers Plus now. Do you want to come too?"

"I'd love to, Cat! I need more nail polish."

She'd *love* it. Now, *that* was music to my ears. "We'll be over in five minutes to pick you up," I said. Finally, something the two of us could do together . . . without you-know-who.

But when we pulled up to Cassidy's, both she *and Shana* came running out of her house. I couldn't believe it!

Cassidy stuck her head in our open car window and said, "I left my jean jacket in the Fitzes' Jeep. Shana just brought it back to me this minute. Can she come with us too?"

I wanted to holler *No!* But I didn't. I plastered a fake smile on my face and replied, "Okay, if she wants." I just didn't want to upset Cassidy in any way.

"Good," said Shana. "I need more glitter lotion."

In monotone mumbles, I introduced Shana to Mom and Lizzie. Then I got out of the car and stalled, shuffling my tennies in the dry brown grass beside the boulevard. I did *not* want to sit next to Shana in the backseat. "You know the rules, Cat," Mom said through thin lips.

"Guests always get the shoulder-strap belts to avoid expensive lawsuits in case of a crash," I mumbled underneath my breath, and climbed in between Cassidy and Shana. Having Shana's hot sweaty arm touch mine felt like getting cozy with raw cow liver. I could tell she thought my sticky bicep was vile too, the way she hugged the door.

As we headed north on Myers Avenue, Shana leaned toward the front seat. "How about some music, Mrs. Carlson?" she asked.

"Mom! No!" I gasped.

Too late. Mom clicked on the station. An oboe and bassoon yawn-a-thon floated over the airwaves. Eerrrgh.

Shana pretended to stick her finger down her throat and made gagging noises. Sheesh. Once again, Cassidy didn't see Shana's mud-flinging. Cassidy wasn't paying attention to anything but her old pink chipped nail polish.

"Could you change the station to KDQB, Mrs. Carlson?" Shana asked.

I nearly swallowed my tongue.

"Is that a station for young people?" Mom replied, cluelessly.

"Uh, yeah." Shana gave a little snort. (Translation: "Like *duh,* lady.")

I was withering in my seat. Melting into a puddle of liquid humiliation.

"I'm afraid that type of music is far too frenetic for my nerves," Mom replied matter-of-factly. "I'm a teacher, Shana. This is a stressful time of year for me. I need soothing music. Isn't this a lovely concerto?" Mom drove one-handed and directed an invisible orchestra with the other hand. But only for thirty seconds tops, of course. My mother would never drive one-handed for long. She was much too sensible.

Shana made more gagging noises.

Lucky thing that Cats like me have nine lives, because I died right there in the backseat.

✳ ✳ ✳

At Savers Plus, Cassidy squealed, "Wow! There's mountains of Milo merch here!"

"Milo's *hot* face is on the front of everything!" Shana shouted. "Thank God for my dad's charge card!" She grabbed a shopping basket and chucked in a Milo Lennox Band pencil pouch, three-ring binder, glue stick, pencil sharpener . . .

Cassidy grabbed a Milo lunch box and held it tightly to her heart.

If I wanted to fit in with these guys, I had to fill my school locker with a bunch of Milo stuff too. I grabbed a shopping basket, jammed it full and hauled it over to Mom.

"Absolutely not," she said quietly. "They cost twice as much as regular school supplies."

"But, Mom," I whined, and launched into a full-scale beg-a-thon.

Mom just shook her head.

Lizzie sighed and said, "What *I* wish I could buy is a telescope, then I could see the International Space Station. Now, *that* would be stratospheric!"

"Oh, *buh-rother*," I snapped, and stomped back down the aisle. Drat, I was stuck with boring non-Milo school supplies!

I could hardly get my paws to cooperate in returning all that Milo stuff to the shelves. I was slooooooowly reaching to put a notebook back . . . when my gaze locked on Milo's glossy image for a long minute. Before, I'd only glanced at his photos high up on Cassidy's walls. But now I was seeing him close, just inches from my own sweaty nose.

Hmm. Milo sure had big brown eyes. Dewy ones, with long eyelashes. And his brown locks were as curly as Greg's. I wondered if Greg was getting ready for school tomorrow, too. . . .

"Oh my *gosh*!" Cassidy screamed.

I jumped and blinked out of my daydream.

"Looky!" Cassidy cried. "Isn't this just *so cuuuute*?" She held up a cotton-candy-pink tank top with spaghetti straps. Milo's face was on the front of it with his name in green letters below his picture. I had to admit it was another great photo of him. His wide smile was as sweet as . . . cotton candy.

"I have to have this top," Cassidy said firmly.

"Ditto." Shana grabbed an identical one and dropped it into her shopping basket.

Oh *no.* Now they were going to own super-cute matching Milo tops—and I wasn't?

I grabbed a tank off the shelf too and leaped over to Mom. I knew what her exact response would be, but I had to try. My mom only liked tasteful neutral tones in clothes. She thought pink was tacky.

Just as I'd predicted, Mom grimaced at the sight of the shirt and whispered, "I don't like spaghetti straps on eleven-year-olds, and I don't like pink on anybody. Come on, Cat. Focus on what you need."

Erg. I *needed* this, but it was useless trying to pry an extra penny from Mom. And I had to save every cent of my own money for a concert ticket. I was just about to give up when Shana said impatiently, "C'mon, let's go pay, Cassidy."

"No! Wait!" I leaped over to them and blurted, "But that shirt costs twelve dollars, Cassidy. I thought you only had enough for nail polish."

Cassidy grinned and said excitedly, "I cut Baird's hair and curled Mom's and Great-Granny's last night when I got home from the cabin. I have enough money to buy polish, the lunch box *and* the shirt!"

"But what about number two pencils and stuff? Don't you need any supplies for school?" I protested. *Please* don't buy matching shirts, I begged silently.

"I've got lots of pens and pencils left over from last year. I hardly use them in school." Cassidy shrugged and smiled.

Shana laughed and said, "Me neither. Why bother?"

I couldn't believe my ears. Sometimes I used up a whole pen in one report, with all the extra-credit pages I usually wrote. Eek. I just knew these guys would reject me if they found out I was a brainiac. I'd be a total dummy not to keep my smarts under wrap at school.

"C'mon, Cassidy," Shana said bossily. "My arms are breaking, carrying all this stuff. Let's go check out."

And I went aaargh, aaargh, aaargh inside. Drat that tight budget and my mom's cluelessness about all things cool!

∗ ∗ ∗

Mom dropped Shana at Cassidy's house after our trip to Savers Plus. "Do you want to come in too, Cat?" Cassidy asked.

"Please, Mom?" I begged.

"For just half an hour, Cat," Mom replied. "Remember, it's a school night."

Shana snickered. I winced.

"It's already five o'clock, Cat," Mom said. "Lizzie and I will buy some groceries, then come pick you up."

When Mom zoomed off, Cassidy grabbed my arm and Shana's and pulled us inside her house and up to her room. "We have to do this fast, guys," she said, "before Cat's mom gets back."

"Do what?" I asked.

"Dye our hair!" she squealed. "So we have cool new looks for school tomorrow."

I choked. "Uh, Cassidy, I don't think so . . . ," I stammered. No way could I ever dye my hair, especially not a bright color. If I did, my mom would have a *cow*!

"I want intense streaks," Shana said, flipping her long hair over her shoulder like some drama major at my dad's college.

I started to chew my fingernails in panic. "I can't do this, Cassidy—"

"Oh, cripes, Cat." Shana snorted. "It's not like Cassidy's suggesting a *mohawk*."

Cassidy giggled and grabbed three packs of Kool-Aid off her dresser top. She waved them under my nose. "Come on, Cat. Pick your fave!"

Shana butted in and grabbed the pack of blueberry Kool-Aid.

"Do you mind if I take the green, Cat?" Cassidy asked kindly. "Then my moptop will match Milo's name on my new shirt. I think that would be cute, don't you?"

I tried to agree but nothing came out of my mouth.

That left me with pink. And I knew how my mom felt about that color.

Ten minutes later, my hair had strawberry streaks. Cassidy's had lime green. And Shana's had blueberry-blue ones. Shana bounced around Cassidy's bedroom, loving her radical new look.

"Oh, Cat," Cassidy breathed. "That is *you*. It makes your cheeks look rosy too. Pretty!"

Pretty?

I peeked sideways at the mirror. Hmm. Maybe Cassidy was right. The flamingo frame around my face did brighten my cheekbones. They looked like a couple of pink carnations. It was actually kind of . . . nice.

Shana stopped admiring herself long enough to mutter, "It's an improvement, Cat."

I knew my mom wouldn't think so. I sucked on a strand of pink hair nervously.

"Here, Puff. Your turn for a new do," Cassidy said. She quickly shampooed and blow-dried him, then grabbed two bottles of nail polish and said, "Let's wait for Cat's mom outside. We can polish Puff's nails while we wait."

On the McDews' front steps, Cassidy and Shana gave Puff a puppy pedicure, polishing his teeny toenails alternating colors—Outrageous Orange and Cha-Cha Cherry Red. I just stood there, having myself a bunch of predinner fingernail appetizers, while I waited for my stressed-out mom.

"I can't believe school starts tomorrow," Cassidy said, beginning to polish her own toenails orange. "I wish life was one long summer. Besides, I can't do math and science and all that stuff with Milo's mug on the brain. No way!"

"Me neither," Shana said, dancing in place on the grass. "I can't blame Milo, though. That's the way I always am in school. I get mostly D's and C's for grades. D's for Don't. C's for Care."

Cassidy giggled.

My eyebrows shot up. If word of my egghead-osity leaked out and Cassidy caught a whiff of it, I knew which direction she'd drift in the friendship department. That was a no-brainer.

Just then Mom's Volvo turned the corner and pulled up to the curb. Lizzie stuck her head out the back window and started to laugh.

Mom leaped out of the car and squawked like a chicken. *"Cat!"* she screeched. *"What in the* world *have you done to your hair?"*

Yikes.

Cassidy giggled.

Shana drawled, "Oh, brother, a freaked-out mother."

"You have school tomorrow!" Mom yelped. *"You . . . you . . . have a new* teacher*!"*

"Mom, calm down," I pleaded, bolting toward the car. "Don't worry. It's just Kool-Aid."

Mom grabbed her chest and let out a breath. "Oh, thank goodness," she gasped. "So it'll wash out."

Shana crossed her arms over her chest. "Well, *I'm* sure wearing my hair like this tomorrow," she said forcefully. "I don't care what teachers think."

Whoa, I thought, my eyes bugging out of my head. Uh-oh.

Cassidy just giggled.

I climbed into the backseat next to Lizzie, and Cassidy called, "Bye, Cat! I just *love* your strawberry-pink hair!"

Mom floored the gas pedal and the Volvo roared toward

home. Eek. Was she speeding? Wide-eyed, I peeked over her shoulder at the speedometer. Five mph *over* the limit. This was *not* my mom at the wheel.

Clearly, she didn't think the girl with the hot-pink streaks in the backseat was her daughter either. "You'll wash that out the minute we get home," she said sternly. "What were you thinking?"

I studied myself in the rearview mirror. I didn't exactly want to face my new teacher looking like a flamingo. But . . . my plain locks weren't a much better alternative.

Suddenly I blurted, "I don't want to wash it out."

Lizzie's mouth formed into a shocked, silent O.

"What?" Mom replied, whipping the Volvo around the corner and up Lucille Street Hill.

"You told me to make new friends," I protested. "So I'm trying. I like Cassidy a lot. And I think she's right. These pink streaks make my cheeks look pretty."

"Oh, Cat." Mom sighed. "You're pretty just the way you are. Now, what would you girls like for dinner?"

And with that, I knew the case was closed.

At home, I watched the last of the pink H_2O disappear down the bathtub drain and I thought, There goes the brand-new me.

8

Slurpable Pie

"**A**t least the baby cubs are cute," I muttered to myself Tuesday morning as I tugged on my Wolves of the Northern Wilderness T-shirt and my non-designer discount jeans. Then I spent five whole minutes trying to smooth my bed head down.

But the combing didn't help my fashion factor a bit, and I felt even worse when I spotted Cassidy and Shana standing together by the front doors of school before first bell. They looked like the Technicolor Twosome with their green and blue streaks, their matching pink Milo tanks and their . . . purple glitter eye shadow. I swallowed hard. Cassidy and Shana were becoming a clique right before my eyes.

Shana looked me up and down, wrinkled her nose and

whispered in my ear, "Very glam, Cat." Another scorcher from Dragon Girl's tongue. That's it, I thought, grinding my teeth. I'm keeping score from now on!

Feeling about as cool as a glass of warm milk, I trudged after Cassidy and Shana into the school and up the stairs to 6A. I saw a million Milo T-shirts in the school hallways, and a gazillion Milo notebooks and backpacks, too. I felt like a big zero, wearing and carrying *no* Milo products.

Then I spied Greg at his locker and instantly felt better. I couldn't wait for Cassidy to meet him. "That boy's in our class, Cassidy," I said quietly, and pointed. "He's really—" *Nice,* I started to say, but before I could finish, Shana stuck her head between ours and piped up, "He looks like a nerd. Can you believe that pile of books he's carrying on the *first* day of school?"

"My gosh, he's a shaggy dog!" Cassidy exclaimed. "He definitely needs a haircut."

"You can't even see his face," Shana said, and snickered. "What's under all that hair, anyhow? A big troll nose, I bet. With warts."

Big beautiful eyes, I thought, as blue as Shana's hair streaks. But I couldn't tell her that. Instead I shook my head and walked into 6A, where, thankfully, Cassidy's desk was right next to mine—and Shana's was way across the room! At least *one* thing was going my way today. I hoped Cassidy and I were true friends and could stay that way, even if we were different, well, types of students.

I peeked over at Greg. I couldn't tell if he was looking at me or not, with all that hair hanging over his eyes. But why would he want to look at me anyway? I was a mess.

I slumped in my seat, still feeling like a big lump of ugliness after Shana's mean remark.

At 9:15, the final bell rang and our new teacher, Ms. Michelsen, said, "It's so good to see this room filled with marvelous sixth graders. . . ."

I smiled at Cassidy, but she was opening and closing her school scissors as she stared at Greg's hair. Hmm. The sight of his shaggy locks was making her scissors-happy.

Ms. Michelsen passed out index cards and said, "Please write your name at the top of the card. Then write anything special I need to know about you, such as if you use an inhaler, or if anything extra-sad or -happy is happening in your life right now. . . ."

I smiled and relaxed in my desk. I loved assignments. I glanced across the room at Shana. She scribbled a few words, then rolled her index card into a microphone. She lip-synched and her feet danced under her desk.

I bent my head over my card and filled up both sides of it, starting with my nickname in big bold letters. I wrote about Annie moving to France and my new friend Cassidy. I wrote about how mad Annie had gotten when I told her about the concert and how I didn't know what to reply to her.

I looked over at Cassidy. Oh my gosh, she was scrawling all over both sides of her card, just like I was. This was *so* exciting!

Maybe Cassidy was a closet top student after all. Maybe she was only pretending that she wasn't—for Shana's sake.

I leaned over and peeked at Cassidy's paper.

Her card said I LOVE MILO LENNOX about twenty times. Cassidy grinned at me and giggled quietly.

I chewed my lip and smiled feebly.

✳ ✳ ✳

At lunchtime, I stood behind Greg in the cafeteria line next to Cassidy and Shana. "Hi, Cat," he said with a smile when he saw me there.

The second Greg spoke, Shana grabbed Cassidy's arm and pulled her away from me.

Erg. Wasn't there anything about me Shana could stand?

Greg stepped closer to me and said quietly, "I heard Ms. Michelsen say your new nickname. I think it fits you. Because your green eyes look like a cat's."

My face caught fire. The second mine did, Greg's did too. "Now I embarrassed you and myself," he said. "I'm such a dope." Then he shot ahead to the milk line before I could reply.

I wondered now if Greg really did like me! I wished I could tell Cassidy about it, but I didn't dare. If word leaked out, I'd be tormented without mercy—by Shana especially.

I moved back in line and joined Cassidy and Shana. "There you are, Cat." Cassidy greeted me as we headed into the cafeteria and found a table. "I thought you were right behind us." At least *someone* had missed me.

Shana just complained, "Six whole hours in this dump,

every day! I should be at home dancing! How am I gonna ace that audition if I don't practice every minute?"

Cassidy murmured sympathetically but I was busy peeking at Greg. He sat alone across the cafeteria, his shaggy head bent over a book as he munched a sandwich. Nobody talked to him and he didn't talk to anybody else. That is, until Judd from 6B walked past him, leaned over and whispered something in his ear. Greg scowled, picked up his book and bag lunch and left in a rush. Judd the Jerk smirked and sat down with his dopey clique of sixth-grade boys.

I hated seeing Greg get bullied, but what could he do? I was as clueless as he was in coping with Nerd Terminators.

I chewed my lip instead of my tuna sandwich. Cassidy wasn't eating her lunch either. She was gazing moon-eyed at Milo's photo on her lunch box.

"I can't even open my lunch box, you guys," she breathed. "This picture of Milo is so hot, I'd burn my fingers on the metal. Sssss." She giggled and swooned. "Oh, I wish I could sit by him at lunch."

And I wished I could sit with Greg and Cassidy. Just the three of us. Shana's scowl could give a girl indigestion.

Everywhere I looked was a sea of Milo Lennox lunch boxes. An ocean of metal Milo faces stretched as far as the eye could see. Even Billie and Brooke had traded their horse boxes for Milo ones. I kept my old scratched-up Animals of the African Savanna lunch box hidden on my lap.

I wanted a Milo lunch box.

I wanted a concert ticket.

I missed Annie.

✳ ✳ ✳

Back in class that afternoon, Ms. Michelsen had us get started on our "What I Did Over Summer Vacation" essays. Instead, Cassidy stuck her frizzy head and entire shoulders underneath the lid of her desk. She took a little tub of fruity blue something or other out of her lunch box. Now she eats, I thought, and smiled. Oh, I was so glad our desks were side by side. Cassidy and I would get super-close! Unlike unlucky Shana way across the room. Ha.

"Is that Jell-O or yogurt?" I whispered.

"Neither," Cassidy whispered back loudly. "It's Blueberry Ooey Gooey Bangs Booster. It tames my mane. You can borrow some if you want. It really works!" she rattled on, even louder. Yikes. I did not want our new teacher to hear her.

Cassidy put a big glob of the blue goop in her hair. She took a comb out of her lunch box and brushed her bangs upward in a dozen super-zealous upsweeps.

Suddenly her bangs were sticking straight up. She looked in a little mirror taped under the lid of her lunch box. She giggled. "Ooooh, did I go overboard, ya think?" she said at full volume, laughing. My stomach flipped nervously. Cassidy was going to get in trouble!

But her skyscraper bangs looked so ridiculous, I couldn't help it. I started to laugh too.

Then Ms. Michelsen was at our side. Oops.

Quietly, without saying a word, Ms. M helped Cassidy clean out her desk. They carried all her things over to an empty desk far away from me . . .

. . . and right next to Miss Nose-in-the-Air Fitz.

Shana smiled sweetly at Cassidy, then smirked back at me. I quickly turned my face away so she couldn't see the dashed hopes in my eyes.

I slumped over my desktop and thought frantically, I *have* to get to that concert somehow. It's my only hope on the horizon of bonding with Cassidy! But who was I kidding? There were only two days left, and no way could I earn enough dough just by walking dogs.

Wait a second. Dough. That was it! A new, even more brilliant moneymaking scheme. I'd have a bake-a-thon! Yes, I'd earn sixty-three big ones quicker than instant pudding! True, I'd never baked anything in my life except one pan of Crispie Crunchie Bars that turned out like concrete, but who had to know?

The holidays were only two months away, so what did everybody need? Pumpkin pie! I'd take preorders and get payment up front, then deliver the goods at Thanksgiving. I'd charge pastry-hungry neighbors five bucks per pie. With that plan in mind, I relaxed and began to concentrate on my essay.

On the playground after school, Shana started practicing her dance moves the second her shoes hit the grass. Excitedly,

I whispered my bake-a-thon idea in Cassidy's ear. "By tomorrow I should have enough cash to score a front-row seat! Oh, I want so badly to come to that concert with you, Cassidy."

"I want you to come too, Cat! Can I help you cook?"

That was *so* nice of her to offer! But I couldn't have her to my house until I lobbied my parents for a major switcheroo—to haul all the literature in my house down to the basement, where it'd be out of sight and wouldn't gross out any nonbooklovers.

"Thanks a lot, Cassidy, but I'll be okay. I've got to go get started. Bye!" I darted away and hurried up Lucille Street Hill alone to my house. It was time to bake a trial pie.

I flung open our front door and tripped right over a humongous pile of library books.

"Sheesh," I muttered, "a girl could break her neck falling over novels in this place." I chucked my backpack onto the couch, then darted into the kitchen to see what Mom had in the cupboards.

Lizzie sat at the kitchen counter, a tall stack of books at her elbow. "I'm starting my third-grade leaf project early for science, Cat," she said. "I'm gathering hundreds of facts on all my favorite trees, you know, ginkgo, horse chestnut, juniper, persimmon, mountain ash—"

"Uh-huh, that's nice. . . ." I dug deep in a cupboard and spied two cans of pumpkin puree. Excellent!

"What are you doing?" Lizzie peered at me through her little wire-rim glasses.

I mumbled the details of my bake-a-thon plan as I dug in the freezer. Ah-ha! A frozen pie shell. Perfect! "Now, what goes inside it?" I wondered aloud, reaching for a cookbook on the shelf above the stove. I found *pumpkin pie* in the index, then found the page. I'd barely glimpsed the convoluted recipe and the long list of ingredients when the doorbell rang.

"Lizzie, would you get the door, please?" I murmured.

"I'm busy. I only have one month to write this report."

"Oh blast." I *tsk*ed and headed for the front door. I reached for the doorknob just as Dad appeared at the top of the stairs. He was carrying an armload of books, obviously busy doing research of some sort too. "Who is it, Cat?" he called down the stairs.

"I don't know, Dad. I'll see."

I threw open the front door and gasped. "Cassidy! Shana!" Eek!

I shut the door in their faces, whirled around and wildly scanned our book-covered house. I quickly shoved the stack of library books on the hallway floor into a corner and threw a raincoat on top of them.

The doorbell rang again. "Dad!" I shouted. "It's just my new friends. Please go back to the study, right now, and take those books with you!"

Dad looked at me like I'd totally lost my marbles. But he shrugged and headed back to the study. Whew.

I opened the front door a crack and said, "Hi."

"We came to help you cook, Cat," Cassidy said. "I know

you're on that tight budget. We'll help stir the dough or some-thing, won't we, Shana?" Cassidy nudged Shana's shoulder.

"I've got an audition in *only* three weeks," Shana grumbled, and gave a mega–eye roll. "I've got to go home and *dance*."

Good. Please leave, I pleaded silently.

"We *have* to help Cat," Cassidy whispered loudly to Shana. "She has money troubles. Cat wants to see Milo live too." Cassidy grabbed Shana's arm and pulled her inside my house. The two pushed past me and headed for the kitchen.

I almost screamed. I dived at the coatrack and grabbed Dad's old tweed jacket with the leather patches on the elbows. I shot forward and held it up high to block Cassidy's and Shana's views of all the bookshelves in our living room.

"Uh, my mom is a *total* neat freak," I lied frantically. "She wouldn't want guests to see our messy house. I'll just cover it up."

"I'm sure your house is fine," Cassidy said sweetly.

But Shana looked at me like I was cuckoo.

On the far side of the living room, I quickly chucked Dad's coat on the floor. I darted ahead of Cassidy and Shana into the kitchen, grabbed a tea towel and threw it over Lizzie's tall stack of tree books. "Hey!" Lizzie yelped in protest.

I narrowed my eyes at her. She took the cue and shushed up.

Then I snatched the open cookbook and whipped it under the table. I could *not* let them see me consulting reference ma-terials of any sort. "Looking things up" would just be too geeky.

Shana huffed, clearly not happy to be a pastry chef assistant. She started to dance in place in the middle of the kitchen, practicing her hip swivels and waist lunges. Lizzie stared at Shana, totally fascinated, like she was watching a tarantula molt or something.

Cassidy spied the cans of pumpkin puree and the frozen pie shell on the counter. "You know, I think I saw my great-granny Rose make a pumpkin pie once," she said, tapping her chin thoughtfully. "I sort of remember what went in it. . . ." She started to dig through the spice cabinet and set a bunch of ingredients on the counter. Boxes of baking soda, baking powder, cinnamon and salt . . . Bottles of molasses, paprika, vinegar, garlic powder . . .

"Are you sure *all* this stuff goes in a pie?" I asked, scratching my cheek hard.

Lizzie peeled her eyes off Shana, who was still bopping in place, and suggested, "Why don't you just look in the cookbook, Cat?"

I whirled around and put my fingers to my lips.

Lizzie hushed. But I knew she was right. I couldn't wing it. There was no way I could make a whole pie without looking at a recipe.

I leaned over, stole a quick peek at the open cookbook lying under the table, then looked away fast. Rats. Did the recipe say half a teaspoon of baking powder or half a cup?

I was ducking down to double-check when Shana said, "Hey, what's down there?"

Uh-oh. If Shana caught me, that would blow the lid right off my cool-girl cover. Before she could look, I quickly kicked the cookbook farther away and squeaked, "Nothing. Just thought I saw a bug."

"Gross." Shana grimaced and went back to her waist lunges. If she bent over any further, she'd have a clear view under our kitchen table, where that cookbook was lurking.

I had to wrap up this trial pie triple-quick and get these guys out of my house! But I knew Cassidy wouldn't leave until she had helped me finish the job; she was just that nice. I opened the cans of pumpkin goop super-fast and scooped it into a mixing bowl.

Cassidy was only too glad to lend her ten speedy fingers. Together, we dumped more stuff in the bowl. I did some guess-work and plopped in a tablespoon of cinnamon and a half cup of baking powder.

Cassidy added little pinches of this and hefty piles of that. I added little squirts of this and big splashes of that. Then we mixed it all up at supersonic speed.

We poured the pumpkin slop into the pie shell and chucked it in the oven. The clock said 4:33 as I set the timer on the oven.

The weird thing was still baking at seven o'clock. It simply would not solidify.

Cassidy and Shana had gone home hours earlier. (I'd sent them out by way of our back door—to avoid the living room bookshelves.)

I bent over the oven and studied that puzzling pie. The orangey-brown goop was still so runny, it sloshed over the edge of the stupid pie shell every time I yanked it out to test it with the stupid toothpick.

It was still baking after dinner. Mom, Dad and Lizzie took peeks at the problem pastry, too. "I hate cooking," I said, frowning at the orange slop.

"Take it out of the oven. Let it cool," Dad suggested.

"Maybe it'll harden up," Mom said.

"Perhaps there is a lesson here for all of us," Lizzie said.

I gave her the beady eye.

"Perhaps not," she said.

An hour later, the little orange lake was still as runny as my nose in midwinter.

"Hey, maybe it's a new concept," Lizzie said. "Slurpable pie." She dug in a kitchen drawer and found a straw. Then she bent over my concoction and took a big suck up.

Lizzie swished the goop around in her mouth for three seconds; then her eyes got all bulbous and crazy. She scrambled to the sink and spat. "Yuck!" she yelled, spitting again. "Gross! Vomit! Barf! That's not pumpkin pie. That's pumpkin *puke*!"

Dad shot me a sympathetic look. Mom's neck got all veiny and stretched out, the way it got when she held her breath, trying not to laugh.

Lizzie took a big gulp of water. "Yeah, Cat," she said with a snort, "you'll get lots of orders for your fantastic pumpkin puke. Everybody in St. Paul will spend Thanksgiving hugging their toilets, throwing up!"

Dad put his arm around my shoulder and said, "You're having a difficult time raising money for this concert ticket, aren't you, Cat? Say, why don't you go to that woodwind quintet concert at our church instead? The performance is coming up in only two weeks, and it's *free*!"

I stared at my clueless dad.

Then I trudged upstairs, muttering, "There is no appreciation for pop culture in this family whatsoever."

Up in my room, I flopped onto my bed and listened to side one of Milo's tape. Okay, I thought, moving slowly to the beat, back to the grindstone. And it would not be a nutmeg or flour one this time, that was for sure.

9

Psycho with a
Capital *S*

"You've got mail," the speakers droned later that night. Another note from Annie. Uh-oh. More angry words, maybe?

I skimmed her short e-mail:

It's been a few days since I've heard from you. My box is totally empty now, compared to the eighteen messages waiting for me last time. Are you mad at me?

I sighed and nibbled a nail. I still felt so confused and sad about her first e-mail, I wasn't sure what to say. I clicked Reply and slowly typed:

No, I'm not mad. . . . I may not even get to that concert anyway. Dog walking just isn't a cleanup cash-wise. Have you been to the Eiffel Tower yet?

I logged off and felt lonelier than ever.

$$* \quad * \quad *$$

Wednesday morning at school, I saw Greg by his locker. He looked so tall and intelligent in his rolled-up sleeves and with his armload of books. Though the millions of pictures of Milo plastered all over the place looked cuter to me every day, he still couldn't hold a candle to the brightest bulb in 6A, Greg Twitchell.

Just then Cassidy ran up to Greg and squealed, "I heard from Julie in 6B that your dad is *manager* at Woodland Arena, Greg! Oh my *gosh*! Does he get free concert tickets?"

My jaw dropped onto the public school linoleum. I couldn't believe what I was hearing. Greg's dad was *manager* at the arena? "Is that true, Greg?" I asked.

He nodded and chewed his lip.

Cassidy grinned at me and winked. Oh no. Greg was sure to be hurt if the first and only time she spoke to him was to get a free ticket. And ten times worse if he thought I'd put her up to it!

I wiggled my head at Cassidy to say a silent no, but she didn't notice.

"How many free tickets does your dad get, Greg?" she asked.

"Two per concert," Greg mumbled, grabbing more books from his locker. "But he gave both of the Milo Lennox Band tickets to my cousins." He turned away from us and dug deeper in his locker for something.

"Too bad!" Cassidy looked at me and shook her head in disappointment. Suddenly Shana danced over, grabbed Cassidy's arm and steered her into class.

Greg pulled his head out of his locker and said quietly, "You know, Cat, fifteen girls have asked me that exact question in the past twenty-four hours. Cassidy is just like all the rest."

"It's not what you think, Greg," I protested. "She's really nice."

He shrugged and marched ahead. Lucky thing he didn't know that Cassidy was trying to get a ticket for me!

It was hard to pay attention that morning, with Greg on my mind and the classroom clock going tick-tock, tick-tock. Time was running out to earn money before tomorrow night!

But I forced myself to concentrate when Ms. Michelsen gave us a fifty-word spelling test. I knew it was a placement test to separate the "regular" spellers from the "challenge" ones.

Shana must've had music blaring in her head, because her body swayed and her neck jerked during the entire test. Cassidy formed imaginary scissors out of two fingers and was making cutting motions as she stared at Greg's shaggy hair. I don't think she even scribbled down half the words.

After lunch, Ms. M handed the tests back. Mine said

"50/50, EXCELLENT!" at the top. This perfect score meant I'd get six extra challenge words per week. I wasn't surprised. I'd been a challenge speller since first grade. I slipped the paper into my folder really fast. It was like a billboard advertising GEEKGIRL GETS BEST GRADE IN CLASS!

Suddenly Shana danced by my desk toward the pencil sharpener. Phew! She hadn't seen my grade. She had started grinding her pencil to a stub near my desk when Greg bounced over and asked loudly, "What score did you get, Cat? Are you a challenge speller too?"

I nearly died! Did Shana have satellite-dish ears? Oh, I hoped not! The pencil sharpener was grinding really noisily. Maybe she hadn't heard him.

I put my finger over my lips but Greg must have been momentarily blinded by his long woolly bangs, because he continued in a megaphone voice, "I don't even have to ask, Cat. I know you're a chal—"

I jumped up from my desk and babbled, "I think Ms. Michelsen's ivy plant needs watering! Right now! Doesn't it look super-thirsty to you, Greg?" Then I dashed across the room to the windowsill and stuck my finger in the potting soil to check for dampness.

I wished I had a muzzle to put on shaggy dog Greg—so he wouldn't broadcast all over school that I was a brainiac. And a couple of pairs of earmuffs, too, to put on Shana and Cassidy—for the whole school year!

I peeked at Greg and smiled weakly. His mouth was hanging open. He shrugged and went back to his desk. Ohhhh, I hoped he didn't think I was too weird!

Before final bell that afternoon, Ms. M handed out spelling word lists. My sheet had twenty words, plus six challenge ones at the bottom. I quickly folded my sheet into a tiny square and stuck it deep in my pocket, out of sight.

"Please review your words every day," Ms. Michelsen said. "We'll have our first spelling test next Wednesday." The bell rang and everybody swarmed around the lockers in the hallway.

Cassidy grabbed her Milo lunch box and pink faux-fur purse. I don't think she even owned a backpack. She stared at her spelling word sheet. "I'm not taking these words home," she muttered, and blew a raspberry. "Looking at a long list of spelling words like this just makes me psycho with a capital *S*!"

I did not correct her spelling, of course. That would be a dead giveaway that I was a nerd.

Cassidy scrunched up her word sheet into a tiny ball and chucked it into her locker. Smiling happily, she said, "Let's go, Cat. Thank God it's almost Friday!"

I sighed. It was only Wednesday.

✳   ✳   ✳

That afternoon I walked two pugs, Wilhelmina and Fred, humming along to Milo's tape on the way. I had practically all the words to "Goddess Caffeina" memorized and half the words to "Me and You Like School Glue." And even though the songs were a little silly, I had to admit, they were very catchy. Before I knew it, I'd walked both dogs and collected two more bucks, making a grand total of thirty-nine now. Unfortunately, it wasn't even close to a hundred dollars.

In school that day I'd heard Shana say, "Hot tickets like Milo's totally sell out the first day they go on sale at Ticket-King."

I turned in at nine o'clock and flip-flopped nervously under my sheet. Time had run out. Chances were slimmer than my bony body that I was going to that concert. Unless some miracle happened between now and tomorrow night, when Cassidy took off for TicketKing in Mr. Fitz's cute Jeep.

✳ ✳ ✳

Thursday morning, I heard about a hundred girls singing Milo's songs (mostly off-key) in the hallways between class. It seemed like every girl in the cosmic universe was going to that concert but me.

The whole day in school, it felt like I had a jawbreaker stuck in my throat.

After school, Cassidy and Shana took off up Carrey Street, all giggly and excited to get their sleeping bags and junk ready for their overnight in the Jeep.

I trudged home alone in my holey tennies. It was bad enough that I couldn't buy a concert ticket and go see Milo with Cassidy. But I also couldn't spend the night with her, nibbling chips, sipping root beer and listening to KDQB on the car radio. When I'd asked Mom about it, she had said exactly what I'd expected:

"Never. Not in a million years. Not on a school night."

And Annie's attempt to comfort me only made it worse. . . .

Don't worry, Cathy. I'm sure you won't miss a thing anyway. That kind of music is such a turnoff. We toured Versailles palace yesterday. Now THAT was fun—and I learned a ton!

I *tsk*ed and pounded out a reply with my pointer finger:

You don't get it, Annie. I WANTED to go!

* * *

The next morning, I stood in the school hallway and sucked on a string of hair nervously while I waited and waited for Cassidy and Shana to show up.

Shana never did make it. Cassidy trudged in after final bell and got marked tardy. She had big black bags under her bloodshot eyes, and her hair looked like an eagle's nest.

"Cassidy," I whispered, grabbing her arm as she passed my desk, "did you and Shana get front-row tickets?"

She nodded and yawned hugely. "We did," she whispered. "But I didn't get a second of sleep. Shana's dad snored all night long."

My shoulders drooped. They were going to Milo's concert without me. Suddenly my heart was hitting rock bottom.

Cassidy slumped into her seat and immediately put her head on her desktop. Ms. M scooted over and tapped

Cassidy's shoulder. Cassidy sat upright, but her head kept flopping forward all morning long.

At lunchtime in the cafeteria, I said gloomily, "Cassidy? I can't go to the concert with you. Even if there are any more tickets left, I don't have enough money to buy one."

Cassidy stared at me with bleary eyes and said in a very slow, sleepy voice, "I feel really bad, Cat. . . . I wish you could go . . . with Shana and me. . . . I thought maybe I could do a bunch . . . more haircuts . . . and give you the money. . . ."

"Really?" I peeped. "That's so nice, Cassidy."

She said through a long wide yawn, "I really . . . wish . . . you could . . . come too, Cat. . . ." Then she put her head down on top of her metal Milo lunch box and fell sound asleep.

I nibbled my tuna sandwich and listened to Cassidy snore.

Just then Greg shuffled by, holding his bag lunch and a carton of milk.

I looked up. "Greg, hi!" I blurted out. He mumbled "Hi" and walked on. Drat, I really *had* hurt his feelings on Wednesday with my bonkers plant-dying-of-thirst excuse.

"Greg, wait!" I said. "Do you want to sit here with me?"

He stopped and turned slightly.

"Please, Greg?"

He nodded, smiled a half smile, then took a seat across from me, next to conked-out Cassidy. Phew! I had another chance.

"Is the nerd terminator home sick today?" he asked, opening his milk and taking a gulp.

I laughed. "Shana's playing hooky." I wished she would every day, so I could sit with Greg. He'd never be sitting here right now if she had been here.

"Tuna, huh?" Greg asked.

"You betcha," I said, munching another bite of my sandwich. "My favorite."

"That figures," he said, and smiled. "All cats like tuna." Oh, I wished I could see his eyes. I bet they sparkled like two freshwater lakes on a blue-sky day. If only I could lean over the table and gently move those sheepdog bangs out of the way . . .

Suddenly Judd the Jerk shot out of nowhere and taunted, "Twitchell's got a girlfriend." Then Judd hissed something in Greg's ear.

Greg tried to swat Judd away but missed. Judd took off laughing and Greg's face turned bright red, the part I could see, anyhow. "What did he say to you, Greg?" I asked.

Greg didn't answer. He just gulped all the milk in his carton, then crushed it in one fist as if it were Judd the Jerk's head.

Wow, Greg sure had strong hands. I felt a little dizzy. I was as crushed as that milk carton.

I woke Cassidy up and dragged her back to class just in time for communications. As Ms. Michelsen wrote on the blackboard, I had a flash of girl genius. Maybe I could call TicketKing and reserve a ticket! That would buy me more time to walk a bunch more dogs.

Humming "Goddess Caffeina," I hurried home as fast as I could after school. I found the St. Paul phone book, looked up TicketKing and dialed the number triple-quick.

"Hi!" I said to the guy on the line. "This is Cat calling from St. Paul."

"Hello, Cat from St. Paul. This is Tony. How can I help you today?"

"Are there tickets left for the Milo Lennox Band concert on September twenty-second?"

"Very few," Tony replied. "And only high up in the bleachers—"

"Oh no!" Now I'd be stuck in the nosebleed section while Cassidy was up front with Shana! Milo would look like an ant at best, and I'd get a headache squinting through binoculars. Plus if Mom and Dad found out my seat was a mile from my chaperone, Mr. Fitz, they might not even let me go!

Well, I had to go, rotten seats or not! I couldn't let Shana have Cassidy to herself doing something *this* fun! Maybe Cassidy and I could meet during the intermission or find some room to stand together. I couldn't give up on my very first fun concert. Besides, I really wanted to see Milo perform his songs live. They were totally growing on me!

"Hello? Anybody there?" Tony said over the line.

"Yes. I'm sorry. Is it possible to reserve a ticket if I don't have quite enough cash at the moment?" I asked weakly.

Tony gave a little laugh. "I'm afraid not. We don't ever

take reservations. Have your mom mail a check or get your pop's plastic, okay? Otherwise, you're out of luck. Bye now." Click.

I gave a mega-decibel sigh, then trudged back upstairs and paced my bedroom floor like a hungry panther. If I couldn't reserve a ticket, how else could I get my paws on one? I had no idea. Oh, I wished I could ask Annie and put her high IQ to use. But she obviously didn't understand.

I called TicketKing again and got put on hold.

By the time a lady finally picked up, ten minutes had passed. "I'm sorry, dear," she said, "the last of the Milo Lennox tickets just sold out."

"No!" I dropped the phone and grabbed my heart. Then I started to cry.

✳   ✳   ✳

The telephone rang at ten o'clock Saturday morning.

"Cat!" Cassidy cried over the line. "KDQB's having a contest to win a free Milo concert ticket. Right now! Do you have a touch-tone phone with a Redial button?"

"Uh, no," I admitted. "All we have at my house are ancient rotary phones from my grandma Victoria's house. My mom and dad like to conserve—"

"Cat!" Cassidy screeched. "Get over to Shana's house right now! If you want to go with Shana and me, here's your chance at a ticket! You can use Shana's cordless telephone! Hurry!"

I ran eleven city blocks in record time. Totally winded, I raced up to Shana's room.

"Here, Cat, quick." Cassidy shoved the Fitzes' phone into my hand. "The second 'Me and You Like School Glue' comes on the radio, hit the Redial button. You *have* to be the first caller if you want to win that free ticket. Got it?"

"Got it." The two of us sat hunched over the radio, our noses inches from the tuning dial. All the muscles in my body were totally taut.

Shana was across the room, dancing madly. She'd barely looked over when I showed up.

The deejay shouted out of the blaring radio, *"Hey, all you girls who didn't get a ticket. Stop crying and cheer up! Keep on listening to KDQB and you'll win a ticket to this* very sold-out *show! We've got just* one *ticket for* you *to win in this next hour. . . ."*

Then another group's song came on the radio. And another. And another.

Twenty minutes passed. No "Like School Glue" yet.

I held the telephone with both hands, my pointer finger hovering over that puny button.

Twenty more minutes passed, as per Shana's digital clock.

And another fifteen. My arms were going numb. I began to lose all feeling in my butt.

Nearly an hour went by and I continued to sit there, my eyes not moving off that itty-bitty button. The music blasted out of the radio. My nerve endings were winding up into super-tight braids. . . .

Suddenly "Me and You Like School Glue" came on the air. *"Now!"* Cassidy screamed.

I leaped out of my skin. I jumped eight feet in the air. I gave that Redial button the jab of the century.

The telephone shot out of my hand. It flew across Shana's bedroom, hit the wall and fell to the floor with a clatter. The batteries popped out and rolled across Shana's rug. All the wires and guts dangled out of that poor dead phone.

Oops. Nobody said anything. Cassidy slapped her hand over her mouth to trap a laugh.

Shana shook her head, stepped over and clicked off the radio.

Finally, I said, "I didn't win, did I?"

10

Tiger Stripes and Leopard Spots

"I'm really sorry I broke your telephone, Mr. Fitz. I could save my allowance for about four weeks and pay you ba—"

"Sack 'em!" Mr. Fitz hollered at the TV. I jumped.

Mr. Fitz peeled his eyes off the football game and grinned at me. "What's that, kiddo?" He saw the mangled cordless telephone in my hand and gave a booming laugh. "It was an old staticky phone anyhow. Chuck it in the garbage, Cat. No problem." He turned back to the TV and bellowed, "Go Vikes!"

Whew. At least somebody in this house was nice.

I trudged back upstairs to say good-bye to Cassidy and Shana. Shana's CD player was blaring Milo's *School Glue* album now and she was back to dancing like mad. Cassidy sat cross-legged on Shana's carpet and was gluing rhinestones onto Shana's red mini and matching top—the audition outfit. I think Cassidy's goal was to cover every square millimeter of the material with costume jewels.

Cassidy kept putting down the glue gun and gawking at Shana. All Shana's practicing was really paying off. I sat down on the edge of the bed to watch a few minutes of her routine—it was just that good.

"I have never seen a better dancer in real life," Cassidy gushed, wide-eyed. "I mean it, Shana, you are getting *so* great!"

Shana stopped mid–hip swivel and said matter-of-factly, "Yup, I'm gonna win that contest. I know I'm good enough." Then, pumped up by Cassidy's buttering up, Shana did a bunch of fancy foot-over-foot moves and deep waist lunges. She kicked and swayed and hopped and weaved all over the room, her long brown hair flying everywhere.

"Goddess Caffeina" began to blast out of the speakers and I started to bounce to the beat. I thought, How *can* a girl sit on her rear with this catchy tune on? Impossible! Suddenly I wanted some flattery from Cassidy, too. Of course, I'd never danced to fast music before, or to any music for that matter. But heck, so what? If Shana could do it, I could too!

I hopped off the bed and started to strut my stuff. I wiggled my hips, snapped my fingers and jerked my long neck. All that twitching sent my glasses sliding down my nose but I just shoved them right back up. I stuck out my thumbs and pitched them over my shoulders, back and forth, back and forth, my arms cranking like a couple of oil well pumps.

Then I added a bony knee-knock move—bang, bang, bang. Hey, I was keeping the beat of Milo's music! Boy, I was rocking. I was on fire!

Cassidy looked at me and started to screech in laughter. "Cat!" she cried. "What is that funky chicken dance you're doing?"

Shana stopped bopping, snorted and said in a disgusted voice, "It's the weird arthritic chicken dance. Who did you take dance lessons from, Great-granny Rose? Someone needs to oil your joints, Cat!"

Oops. I'd sure botched *that* fandango. I quickly plastered on a fake grin. "I was just kidding around! Now here's my gorilla dance. Ooo—ooo—ooo." I stuck my hands in my armpits and made like an ape doing the mambo.

Cassidy laughed and jumped up. "Teach me, Cat!" she begged.

A minute later, Cassidy squealed as Shana did a perfect handstand.

I sighed and nearly finished off a whole fingernail. Everything about Shana was cool in Cassidy's eyes. She danced cool, dressed cool . . . wait a second. At least I could buy some new clothes now. Since I wouldn't be spending money on a ticket after all, I had thirty-nine bucks! But I definitely needed Cassidy's help picking out clothes. I wouldn't know where to begin.

I whispered in her ear, "Can you go with me to Resurrection Duds today?"

Cassidy looked at the project in her lap, then whispered back, "I promised Shana I'd make this, but . . . I suppose I could go for a *little* while and help you pick out some glam things. You know how much I love shopping for clothes."

Cassidy set down the glue gun and told Shana she was going with me. I felt so excited, my heart started to do the foxtrot!

Shana's hands flew to her hips. "Cassidy!" she protested. "You promised you'd help with my *outfit,* my *hair,* my *nails,* my *shoes,* my *makeup*! There's tons to do in only two weeks!"

Cassidy twirled a strand of her frizzy hair around her finger and replied calmly, "I know, Shana. But I told Cat I'd go to Resurrection Duds with her last week. I'll only be gone a teensy little bit, then I'll be right back, okay? I'll help you win that contest, Shana. And you *will* win, don't worry!" She smiled sweetly.

"Okay. Hurry back, Cassidy." Then Shana glared at me and went back to dancing.

Cassidy and I took off together down Barrymore Street. Oh, this was heaven! Just the *two* of us, alone on a sunny warm September morning—without Shana! I couldn't believe Cassidy had disagreed with Shana. I wished *I* could, but I didn't dare get completely on her bad side—or I'd be booted out of the threesome for sure.

I couldn't let Cassidy inside my literature-filled living

room, so I ran into the house alone to get my money. And soon, we were skipping up Lucille Street Hill, my wad of cash stuffed in my bibs pocket. At Myers Avenue I got up the nerve to ask, "Do you, um, think Shana is . . . bossy?"

Cassidy shrugged. "Oh, not really," she said, and smiled. "I think she's just focused on winning that contest. And she's going to win. That's so cool!"

I munched another fingernail and sighed quietly. Would I ever measure up to Shana in Cassidy's eyes?

Outside Resurrection Duds, Cassidy said, "Now *you* need to focus, Cat. Close your peepers. Focus on . . . fashion. What do you want your clothes to say about you to the kids at school?"

I shut my eyes and thought hard. Hmm, my clothes . . . making a statement. I wanted them to say . . . that I was not a nerd . . . that I could be cool too . . . that I was . . .

"One cool Cat!" I exclaimed, my eyes popping open.

"Oh, I love it. I can see it too!" Cassidy grabbed my arm and pulled me into Resurrection Duds. We whipped through the racks of old clothes, sneezing our heads off from the dust. "Here's a great top!" she said. "It looks like your size."

I grabbed it.

"Omigosh," Cassidy gushed, "these glitter pants are awesome too. I bet they'd fit you."

I draped the top over my arm and grabbed the glitter pants.

Cassidy dug through the barrels of old shoes and boots.

"Oh, I looooove these boots, don't you?" she breathed. "They're size eight."

"Nearly my size!" I cried, and hugged them to my chest. I marched up to the checkout counter with my armload of stuff. The clerk was reading *Lowdown on High Fashion.* She looked up from her magazine and said to me, "Better try those things on before you pay, sweetie. All sales final."

"Okay." I turned toward the dressing room.

"I better get back and help Shana now," Cassidy said, "before she gets mad."

My shoulders drooped. Drat. I wished Shana didn't have to hog Cassidy every minute. I wished I were cool enough that Cassidy would stand up to Shana and say she wanted to spend *more* time with me. But at least Cassidy had helped me pick out this stuff.

"Are you sure you really like these things?" I asked.

"I *love* them! This was fun. Bye, Cat!" And Cassidy took off.

I slipped into the dressing room and yanked off my old bibs and T-shirt. I tugged on the pants, top and boots, coughing like crazy from the dust.

I studied myself in the dressing room mirror and tried to imagine what Cassidy would say. I turned around slowly in the purple platform boots (only one size too big—I'd grow into them—and hardly scuffed at all), shiny glitter purple tiger-stripe pants (just one tiny tear, on the left leg) and a bright green velour leopard-print top (only two grease spots—blending in with the leopard spots—at the neck).

"These clothes are *purrrrr*fect for my cool-Cat theme," I whispered to myself, and whistled quietly. "This is the new me. Where have I been all my life?"

I gazed in wonderment at the Cat Print-cess in the mirror for another minute. Then I changed back into my old bib shorts and hauled my treasures to the checkout counter.

"I'll take all this stuff, please," I told the lady. She wore a pink nametag that said DOLORES, AT YOUR SERVICE.

"You betcha, sweetie," Dolores said, and cracked her gum.

I skipped home with my new (used) clothes and boots in a plastic bag, thinking, This stuff will definitely, successfully, combat nerd syndrome. From now on, there will be no more fashion *faux paws* for this Cat!

And I even had enough money left over for a Milo Lennox Band poster. I'd buy it that day at Paper Mart and invite Cassidy over to see it soon—the minute I rearranged our house so it didn't look like a public library.

At home, I chucked the shopping bag in my closet, then begged Dad to drive me to Paper Mart. He finally agreed, since he needed more pens and manila envelopes.

By dinnertime, I had a *life-size* poster of Milo Lennox taped to my bedroom wall. Gosh, the longer I stared at Milo holding his cool yellow guitar, the more I had to agree with Cassidy and the other girls at Lewis Elementary . . . this curly-haired superstar had one beauteous mug. Not as cute as Greg Twitchell, granted, but quite the hottie, as Cassidy would say.

On Sunday morning, I opened my e-mail box and found a note from Annie. I gulped and read:

I guess this means I won't be hearing from you anymore. You've found fun new friends to hang out with and new hobbies to do without me. I won't have time for e-mail anyway with all the homework they're giving me here. . . . But I really want you to know that I'm sorry I hurt your feelings and that I totally loved our eleven years together. I only wish it could be eleven times eleven. Au revoir, Annie
P.S. If you change your mind, I promise to write back as soon as I dig myself out of this pile of work and can check e-mail again.

She apologized! I smiled, clicked Reply and quickly pecked:

You'll ALWAYS be my friend, Annie, even if we don't agree on everything. No one can replace you!

I wrote her about my new outfit, wished her luck with school and told her how happy I'd be to hear from her when she had more time. Then I logged off and called Cassidy.

"She's not home. Cassidy's helping Shana with some audition duds all day," Baird said.

But amazingly my spirits stayed buoyed. Because in spite

of a whole ocean separating us, I felt close to Annie again—even if I wasn't ready to tell her everything about life at home yet. And tomorrow when I'd be wearing cool new clothes to school, I'd be as hip as Shana Fitz, for sure.

✳ ✳ ✳

Monday morning, I leaped out of bed, tugged on my animal-print top and pants and had a coughing fit. "Maybe I should have washed this stuff before I put it on," I murmured to myself. "Too late now. My new non-nerd image can't wait another twenty-four hours."

I yanked on the platform boots and instantly felt like a human skyscraper in the gargantuan heels. Fabulous. I'd be *so* imposing!

Then I tried to stretch out the velour sweater a little bit at the neck. I'd probably bake at school wearing this thick fuzzy top. Oh, well. Discomfort due to overheating was a small price to pay for coolness.

I clomped out to the hallway in my huge platform heels just as Lizzie padded out of her room in her bunny slippers. *"Cat?"* she screeched. *"You* are wearing the *pelts* of poor dead gorgeous *animals*?"

"Lizzie," I replied calmly, shaking my head, "would you please put on your glasses? I am wearing strictly vinyl and polyester. Zero bona fide animal skins. *Relax*." Then I clomped downstairs in those colossal soles to find Mom and Dad.

They were both standing in the middle of the living room. Mom had an armload of students' papers she was trying to stuff into her briefcase. She glanced over at me, gave a loud yelp and threw up her arms.

Papers flew all over the room. Dad stared at me and scratched his bald head.

Mom reached over and took hold of Dad's arm to steady herself. Wow. I was such a knockout that I'd knocked the wind right out of my mom!

She smiled weakly and murmured to Dad, "We're entering uncharted territory, Carl. I feel I've lost my compass. . . ."

"Look here, Cat," Dad said, "you can't go to school looking like neon rain forest roadkill." Mom elbowed Dad's round belly.

I *tsk*ed and said firmly, "Dad, you are stuck in the cultural dark ages. I am cool."

"Perhaps it's not wise to engage in a wardrobe war at this juncture, Carl," Mom muttered.

"Perhaps you're right, Elsa," Dad muttered back. "It could backfire."

I left them to their muttering and clomped into the kitchen. I munched my Crispie Crunchies and thought, What do my parents know? Nothing. I love it when critics are proven wrong by mass appeal. I'll *wow* the kids at school. I'll show my clueless family.

Half an hour later, I struck a pose by my locker at school, waiting for Cassidy to show up for first bell. I felt ten feet tall and like a total supermodel. Just then the horse freaks Billie and Brooke came tromping down the hall in their cowboy boots. They pointed at me, bent over double at their rawhide belts and hooted their heads off.

What in heck was the matter with those guys? Were my tiger-stripe pants unzipped or something? I looked at my clothes. No.

Then Shana danced down the hall, laid her big brown eyes on me and did a huge belly laugh. "Cat Carlson!" She guffawed and gave an arrogant toss of her long brown hair. "You are *so* style impaired!"

I was shaking my head in total confusion when suddenly Cassidy jumped through the crowd, grabbed my arm and hauled me into the girls' bathroom. Then, faster than you can say "fashion crisis," she pulled me into a stall and quickly locked the door behind us.

"Cat," she whispered, "I didn't think you'd wear the leopard top and the tiger pants *together*. *Plus* the boots!"

Huh? I'd felt like a towering alp, but now I seemed to be shrinking—down to about a molehill.

"They're separates, Cat. They don't all go together," Cassidy went on in a whisper. "I thought you knew."

"Oh," I said, shrugging helplessly.

"Come to my house after school, Cat," Cassidy said quietly. "I'll loan you a top that will look cute with those pants. You can borrow it until you're off that tight budget. You could also wear the leopard top with your blue jeans for another cool outfit."

Cassidy said *cool*. "Thanks, Cassidy! I can't wait until three-thirty."

But I had to wait. That Monday was the longest school day in the history of girlkind. I was so preoccupied in class that I forgot my brainiac cover. My hand floated up in the air, an old automatic habit whenever a teacher asked a question. In the olden days, Annie and I even waved both our hands wildly in the air, to double our chances of teachers calling on us.

"Yes, Cat?" Ms. Michelsen looked at me and smiled. "Do you know the answer?"

I peeled my eyes off my embarrassing outfit. Yikes! What in the world was my hand doing in the air? I quickly yanked it back down and sat on it.

Everybody was staring at me, including Shana. (Actually, Cassidy wasn't; she was fiddling with her barrettes.)

I shook my head and shrugged. Ms. M looked disappointed. Rats, I didn't like disappointing my nice new teacher. But I put both hands under my legs to keep them from going up . . . in case my old habit tried to rise again.

11

C for Cardiac Arrest

"**T**oo microscopic on me," I said, and laughed. My long arms hung out of Cassidy's little blue cap-sleeve top like an orangutan's. Half of my belly stuck out too.

Cassidy giggled. "Here, Cat. Try this tank and this tee. They're too big for me."

I tried them on, one at a time, feeling *so* glad to be at her house after school without you-know-who. Both of the tops looked terrific with the tiger-stripe pants. The tank was bright yellow, Milo's favorite color. The tee was flamingo pink and had a tiny green palm tree on the pocket. "Are you sure I can borrow two shirts, Cassidy?" I asked, my heart doing about five somersaults.

"Totally sure. Take this too, Cat." She handed me a clear box filled with sparkly bright barrettes and hair bands. "They're extras. I don't need them right now."

"Omigosh, Cassidy. Thanks. I just *love* this stuff."

But my mom didn't.

When I showed her the tops at dinnertime, she said, "Oh goodness, pink again? And you can't wear the yellow shirt to school, Cat. It's too skimpy."

I gave a major huff and marched to my room. With Mom as my style guide, it was no wonder I was forever lost in Geekdom!

Okay then, I wouldn't wear the teensy tank to school. But Cassidy's other top? Definitely. "Because," I muttered to myself, sticking out my chin, "I just decided that pink is *my* favorite color."

The next morning, Mom had already left for work when I pulled on Cassidy's pink tee and my tiger-stripe pants. Then I focused on *hair.*

Cripes, bed head had become a chronic dilemma lately. (Or had it always been and I just hadn't noticed? Hmm.) I grabbed my hairbrush and pounded at my scalp for *fifteen* full minutes. Success! I flattened most of the cloud-touching mountain ranges. But now dozens of limp strings dangled in my face. I took all the pink and purple barrettes out of Cassidy's box and clipped my linguini hair back behind my ears. Three barrettes per side.

I'd never worn my hair back from my face before, except

for the whale-spout ponytail Cassidy gave me. It looked . . . pretty? I think maybe so.

At school at 9:05, I was chucking my stuff in my locker when Greg stepped up to me and said quietly, "You look nice today, Cat."

Who knew that a cool look could make a girl's face catch fire? I went all dizzy and flushed and murmured, "Thanks, Greg!"

Then Cassidy showed up, smiled widely and winked at me.

I floated into 6A, defying gravity in those ten-pound soles! For the first time ever at Lewis Elementary, I felt fashionably confident and borderline beautiful.

I sashayed to my desk and took a seat. I gingerly touched my barrettes, making sure they were staying put. All was peachy-pink. Until . . .

Shana danced by my desk. She did a double take at me, then put her poison-glossed lips up to my ear. "What'd you do? Raid Cassidy's room?" She snickered. "You're trying to be just like her, copyCat. But you'll never be cool without Cassidy's help. Wannabe." Shana snorted, then strode away.

My shoulders went all concave on me. I felt my heart go bump, bump, bump, knocking down about a dozen notches on the Happy Meter.

Was Shana right? Probably. Without Cassidy, I had little hope of ever finding my way out of the Nerd Labyrinth I'd been lost in for eleven years.

* * *

After recess, I was still trying to recover from Shana's venomous snakebite when Ms. Michelsen said, "Please turn in your summer vacation essays now. And remember that your first book reports are due this Friday."

I moved into line at Ms. M's desk to turn in my essay. I rolled my masterpiece into a tight scroll so Cassidy and Shana couldn't see that it was ten pages thick. I guess I got carried away writing all about my best friend moving to Paris.

Shana slipped into line beside me and I spied her essay. Wow, it was only four *lines* long. I quickly stuck mine behind my back.

"Whatcha hiding there, Cat?" Shana's eyes got all squinty.

"Nothing."

She stared at me ultra-suspiciously, as if she had X-ray vision and could see right through my new cool clothes to the inner nerd underneath.

Quickly, I stuffed the paper down the seat of my tiger-stripe pants.

I held up my empty hands, palms opened wide. "Zilch," I said. "See?" Then I muttered, "Excuse me," and started walking backward to my desk, hiding my lumpy rear from Shana's gaze. I'd turn the essay in later, on the sly, when Shana wasn't looking.

I sat down on my crinkly rump and squirmed for nearly an hour during math, until Ms. Michelsen finally gave us a bathroom break. Who knew that hiding the real brainy me would be this uncomfortable?

* * *

After school, Cassidy took off to Shana's house to help with the diva suit some more. Frantically, I watched them head across the schoolyard together. I just hated the idea of hanging out with Dragon Mouth, but I wanted to spend more time with Cassidy! Plus, I honestly wanted to help prep for the concert, even though I wasn't going to it. I didn't want to be left out of every cool thing. I had to weasel into Shana's plans somehow, even if it meant getting torched again by her fire breath.

I tromped up Carrey Street in my behemoth boots and caught up to them.

"I'll help whip that audition suit into shape too, Shana," I offered. "I'll even make the 'I love you, Milo' signs you guys want to carry at the concert," I added desperately. Sheesh, my name was Cat, but I sure felt like a little puppy wagging its tail, the way I was pleading.

Shana huffed, narrowed her eyes and said, "All right. But don't break anything, Cat, or you'll set back the schedule."

"Okeydoke," I said brightly.

But at Shana's house I accidentally spilled a can of Coke on her rug. Cassidy scrambled to the bathroom for a sponge while I quickly dabbed at the puddle of pop with a tissue.

"I'm calling you Klutzilla from now on," Shana spat, dancing past.

Ooohhh. Now I was a klutz, too. How many more toxic names was Miss Torpedo Tongue going to shoot at me? Well, I had no choice but to bite my own tongue. I didn't dare tell her off.

Cassidy came running back and helped mop up the mess.

Just then, Shana came dancing past again and tripped over my long legs. "Cat!" she hollered. "If I break a leg, I'm *out* of the contest!"

"I'm sorry," I peeped, shrinking like a squeezed-out sponge.

Cassidy whispered in my ear, "Don't feel bad, Cat. Shana's just stressed out." Then Cassidy turned to Shana and said in a soothing voice, "Don't worry. You're going to win. *You are.*" The halo of frizz around Cassidy's face made her look angelic at that moment. Her mellow voice worked like magic on Shana's nerves. Shana's tight fists relaxed and Cassidy went on, "Even if you had a broken leg, Shana, you'd still win. You're just that good."

Shana sighed mega-dramatically and said, "I know. But the problem is the competition! If I could just show Milo how great I am before he sees the other girls dance, I know he'd say, 'Don't bother auditioning the rest. Here's our winner right here—Shana Fitz!' "

Hmm. My fingers started to rub my chin. Maybe I could figure out a way to land Shana an early-bird audition. If I did her a favor that huge, maybe she'd be able to stand my guts a little more and let me tag along when she and Cassidy did fun stuff. Think, think, I ordered my brain. How to get Shana up to see Milo ahead of the pack? It was time to put my egghead to work and hatch a plan.

* * *

On Wednesday I glued on a gazillion rhinestones and even took home the concert signs to work on after dinner. I hoped I was earning a few bonus points with Shana, though the sight of me still seemed to nauseate her.

At eight o'clock that night, I sat cross-legged on my bedroom floor, printing I LOVE YOU, MILO in perfect, supersize neon pink letters on poster board. I was listening to side one of Milo's cassette for about the twenty-fifth time. I hadn't even listened to side two yet, but I would . . . as soon as I knew all of side one by heart. My butt bopped to the beat and I bit my lip in concentration as I wrote MIL—

"Cat!"

I looked up. Dad was waving his arms at me.

I yanked off the headphones and smiled. "What, Dad?"

"Have you done your homework for tomorrow?" he asked.

"Not yet. But I will."

"Cat," he said firmly. Dad had that "concerned father" look on his face. "If your grades nose-dive, Mom and I will have to separate you from Cassidy and Shana."

My heart skipped a beat. Eek. Dad wouldn't do that . . . would he? If I got completely separated from Cassidy, she'd spend every free second doing fun stuff with Shana. My friend*ship* with Cassidy would be a sunken wreck!

"Don't worry, Dad," I replied nervously, "I'll get to my homework."

But I didn't. Dad left the room and I bent right back over those signs. For the first time since first grade, I left my backpack lying on my bedroom floor, untouched. "It can't hurt if I let my homework slide for one little day," I murmured. "No one will know."

Thursday night after dinner, I worked on the signs again. Shana wanted them done triple-quick and I was on top of the task. "I'll do my homework just as soon as I finish this last one," I whispered to myself. "I'll squeeze sideways into this cozy clique yet!"

But I did such an A+ job on the lettering that I forgot all about schoolwork.

First thing Friday morning, Ms. Michelsen said, "Please hand in your book reports now."

Oh no! I'd totally forgotten to write it! Wide-eyed, I watched kids line up at Ms. M's desk to pass in their reports. I grabbed a piece of paper and a gel pen and did a frantic three-second brainstorm. Pick a book, Cat, I ordered myself, any book. Um, *Charlotte's Web*.

Okay. I read it in second grade and vaguely remembered the plot. What was it about again?

I madly scribbled across the lined paper:

Charlotte's Web
Book Report by Cat Carlson
There was a trio of delightful characters in this spellbinding book: a pig, a girl, a spider. Charlotte was no ordinary spider, oh no. She was a writer and a challenge speller, no less. The setting? A barn. Charlotte's writing instrument? Her web.

I glanced up. Ms. M was looking at me. She smiled warmly, probably thinking I was putting finishing touches on my report. But in truth, I was putting *beginning* touches on it. Yikes.

With slumped shoulders, I carried my puny report to the front of the room and set it on her desk. I slunk back to my seat and munched on a fingernail. Never had I *ever* forgotten a homework assignment. Not once since kindergarten. What was *wrong* with me? My parents would freak if they found out.

I crossed my fingers and toes and wished like crazy that Ms. M would love the three lines I wrote and give me a good grade.

Just then, Ms. M called Cassidy and Shana up to her desk. I heard Ms. M say quietly, "The book reports were due today, girls, remember?"

I quickly tiptoed over to the globe near Ms. M's desk and pretended to look at Europe. The globe table was a perfect spy post within earshot of her desk.

In a mouse whisper, Ms. M asked Shana where her paper was. Shana shrugged and did ceiling patrol with her eyes. Ms. M did not look pleased. She turned to Cassidy. "And where is your report?" Ms. M asked quietly.

I peeked sideways at Cassidy. Her eyes were super-wide. I could tell she felt nervous. And I knew what happened to Cassidy when she got nervous. Sure enough . . .

"My homework ate my dog," Cassidy blurted out.

Ms. M's jaw dropped. Shana's hand shot to her mouth and her shoulders started to shake with silent laughter.

Ms. M looked stupefied. She said in a low voice, "We'll discuss this after school, girls. Please take your seats."

Cassidy and Shana scurried to their desks. "This is no laughing matter, Shana," Cassidy whispered, giggling.

✳ ✳ ✳

"Yeah, Cassidy's here," Shana said grumpily over the phone Saturday morning when I called. "She'll be here *all day,* planning my audition hairdo and stuff. We're busy, geek. Bye."

Geek.

The saltwater pools behind my eyes filled up and splashed over the banks. I could barely see to slip the cassette into the Walkman. I put the headphones on and headed up the street to walk the two pugs, Wilhelmina and Fred. Even though it was too late to buy a concert ticket, I figured it couldn't hurt to have some extra money of my own to spend on clothes.

I gave a loud sniff and was digging in my bibs pocket for a Kleenex when all of a sudden, a song I'd never heard before began to play. I looked down at the Walkman, and sure enough, I'd accidentally put side two on by mistake.

Before I could flip the tape over, Milo started to sing in a soft sweet tenor, "Cute little nerdgirl ... So busy in the library ... Studying the glossary ... Memorizing history ... Can you take a minute ... And think about me? ... Cute little nerdgirl ... Can't you see? ... Cute little nerdgirl ... You're the one for me."

What?

I wiped my nose on the back of my hand and quickly

rewound the tape. Not moving from that spot on the sidewalk, I listened to "Cute Little Nerdgirl" again. I couldn't believe it. This superstar had a soft spot in his heart for a brainiac! A brainiac like me. I played the song another time.

And again.

And over and over as I walked the pugs.

I hummed "Cute Little Nerdgirl" all afternoon. "Now I really wish I were going to your concert," I whispered to Milo's poster. "If I were, I'd get up close to the stage and tell you how much I like this song. It really made a dark day sunny for me, Milo. Thanks."

On Sunday, I didn't even bother to call Cassidy because Dad made me get right at my homework. I sat at my desk but it wasn't easy focusing on fractions with Milo's life-size poster right there. It was like the red-hot celebrity was looking straight at me, I swear.

Humming my new favorite song, I started to draw a free-hand map of the continents for my social studies homework. We were supposed to do it from memory, based on our review in class. I began to draw the landmasses but my eyes kept drifting over to the poster. My pencil continued to move across the page while my eyes stayed locked on the magnificent Milo.

After a few minutes, Lizzie strolled into my bedroom and took a gander at my homework. "What in *heck* have you done to Australia?" she gasped.

I peeled my eyes off the melodious Romeo and looked down at my map.

Oops. I'd accidentally drawn a full head of gorgeous curly hair all over Australia. It was Milo, I think. No, wait. The hair was too long. I'd drawn . . . Greg. Huh.

Lizzie grabbed a pencil off my desktop and added a mouth. She shook her head and said, "I can't believe you turned a beautiful continent like Australia into a boy. You know what I think? I think boys are like slugs. They serve some purpose but it's hard to imagine what."

✳ ✳ ✳

On Monday morning, Ms. Michelsen handed back our graded book reports. I blinked three times but still wasn't sure I was seeing things right. A big ugly C- sat on top of the page.

A large lump crept into my throat, lodged there and stayed all morning.

I spent recess hidden in a bathroom stall. I'd never gotten a B in all my life, much less a C. And a C-*minus* to top it off.

C for Cry, which was what I did. Very quietly, in that bathroom stall.

C for Cardiac Arrest, which was what would happen to my parents when they saw this paper. Well, they wouldn't see it. I'd hide it.

After recess, Cassidy studied me closely in the hallway. "Cat?" she said quietly. "Where were you at recess? I was looking for you. Have you been crying?"

"I think it's allergies, Cassidy," I lied, doing a pretend sniff. "Maybe as a Cat I've become allergic to myself."

Cassidy giggled. I didn't.

At home after school, I tore that C- paper into a pile of tiny pieces. I hid them behind some giant dust bunnies under my bed. I couldn't put the paper bits in a garbage can in the house, or Eagle-eye Mom would find them. I'd throw the pieces in the trash can outside by the garage on Thursday. The garbage truck always came early Friday mornings.

Coughing from the dust, I crawled out from underneath my bed. Then I dived at my desk and got to work. I had to redeem myself in Ms. M's eyes and quick.

This Cat worked like a dog on homework before and after dinner. I even made my current-events sheet five pages long instead of one.

❊ ❊ ❊

Tuesday morning, I turned in my five-page extra-credit sheet on the sly when Cassidy and Shana weren't looking.

After lunch, Ms. Michelsen handed it back to me with a pat on the shoulder and a big smile. My paper had a giant A+ at the top with EXCELLENT! and 25 EXTRA-CREDIT POINTS in screaming green letters.

Phew. I was back on track. I felt so relieved that I forgot to hide the good grade. Suddenly Shana danced by my desk and went, *"Whoa! Twenty-five extra-credit points?"*

I quickly shoved the paper into my desk, but it was too late. Shana leaned down and jeered in my ear, "I knew it. From the day I met you. You *are* a total *nerd*." Shana made a face and looked thoroughly grossed out.

I cringed. I crumpled up.

I was doomed. I just knew Shana would tell Cassidy!

"Shana, wait." I grabbed her arm. She gave a little shudder as if she'd just been slimed by geek germs. I let go and whispered frantically, "I'll get you an early-bird audition for that dance contest, *if* you promise not to tell Cassidy about this ace grade."

"An early tryout? How?" Shana demanded.

"I've got ideas," I lied. "Do you promise you won't tell Cassidy?"

Shana nodded, then started to bop on her toes excitedly. "I'm counting on you, Cat," she said. "Don't let me down, or else your nerd secret won't be safe anymore."

"Okay." I chewed my lip nervously. One early-bird audition, coming right up. Gulp.

12

Pile of V.I.P. Passes

"**H**ow do people get backstage at concerts?" I whispered into Cassidy's frizzy hair during gym Tuesday afternoon. "I heard something about that on MTV at Shana's."

Cassidy whispered in my ear, "With backstage passes. They're also called V.I.P. passes."

"How does somebody get one of those?" I asked quietly.

"People who work at stadiums get passes." Suddenly Cassidy's eyes popped wide open. "Greg! He could get a pass from his dad!"

I grinned and whispered, "That's perfect! I'm going to try to get one for Shana. Then she can go straight to Milo's dressing room and audition there, before the other girls do out front. I'll try to get passes for you and me, too, so we can see Milo together backstage!"

Cassidy's jaw practically fell onto the gym floor. She whispered in my ear, "I'm *so* excited!"

"Me too," I whispered back.

Then we crossed our arms and legs, and hoped this scheme would fly.

✳ ✳ ✳

After school, I gnawed several fingernails to nubs, waiting for Greg to get his week-in-the-wilderness-size backpack stuffed with all his calculators and reference books and stuff.

Finally, he loped down the hallway and out of the school, alone as always. I trailed him at a safe distance so Judd the Jerk wouldn't see us together and jeer at us. Kicking through piles of red and yellow leaves, I thought, *Now* they turn color and fall off the trees. Two weeks too late to get a raking job. A block from school, I called, "Hey, Greg!"

He turned around and grinned hugely when he saw me.

I clomped across the street and tripped on the curb. Oops. I just couldn't get the hang of walking in those king-size clodhoppers, and it didn't help that they were one size too big. But I sure loved how great they looked.

"Hi, Cat!" Boy, Greg seemed super-pleased to see me. He bounced from foot to foot in his loafers. "What's up?"

"Um, I was thinking about the science fair, Greg," I lied.

"The school science fair next February? Do you have an idea for a project already? I do," Greg rattled on excitedly.

"I'm using recyclables again. I'm going to power a homemade motorized scooter with the methane from rotting rutabagas and cabbage leaves—"

"Oh!" I said. "That sounds excellent. Can I come see what you're working on?"

Greg's face turned autumn-maple-leaf red, the part of his face I could see, anyway. "You mean . . . *you* come to my house, Cat?"

I nodded eagerly.

"Uh, sure! Great!" he said. So we marched up Carrey Street and Greg continued to explain how his project worked.

It sounded complicated—and impressive. "How do you keep track of it all?" I asked.

"It's hard," Greg replied. We turned the corner and were heading up the block to his house when he added matter-of-factly, "I could sure use another set of hands for all the work, Cat."

I gulped. "Are you asking *me*? To be your science fair project partner?"

Greg nodded on a motorized neck.

Wow, this would practically be like working with Einstein! Only, Greg was about a million times cuter than Einstein. The thought of working with him gave me weak-knee syndrome. And it was totally fantastic because now I'd have daily opportunities to search his house for some golden slips of paper— V.I.P. passes to Woodland Arena!

"Yes!" I agreed. "I'll be your project partner. Let's go check on those rotting rutabagas right now!"

Greg flew up his front steps and threw open the door. Grinning like a Cheshire cat, I followed him inside. And there I was, entering the Twitchells' house. Yesss! Moving full speed ahead with Operation Score-a-Pass!

I dropped my backpack on a chair in the hallway, then clomped after Greg into the kitchen, where he introduced me to his mom. She was a little on the tubby side and as sweet as the lemonade she offered us. Greg led me down the hall and out the back door to the garage.

"This is my laboratory," he said with a wide sweep of his arm.

"Wow!" I stepped inside and gave a quiet whistle. The next second, my fingers flew to my nose and pinched my nostrils shut. P.U.! It smelled like a dirty garbage disposal in there.

Greg handed me a clothespin. "Here, Cat, put this on," he said. "I started the experiment in the basement but it stunk up the house so bad, Mom made me move everything out here. I'm so used to the smell now, I don't even notice it anymore."

I clipped the clothespin on my nose. Ouch. But at least my gag mechanism calmed down.

Totally awestruck, I scanned Greg's laboratory. Hoses ran everywhere between garbage cans filled with rotten vegetable goop. Boxes of rutabagas were stacked next to a small scooter with a mini–methane tank under the seat. Dried-up cabbage leaves and other junk littered the floor, and dozens of books, propped open with screwdrivers and hammers, lay on the workbench.

"This is better than *Mad Science* on TV, Greg! So," I squeaked through my pinched nostrils, "does your dad help with your experiments when he's home, or is he too busy with work he brings home from Woodland Arena in his *briefcase*?" I didn't waste a minute starting to snoop for clandestine information.

"My dad doesn't usually have time to help me," Greg replied absentmindedly. He slipped on a pair of safety goggles and studied a gauge. "He brings paperwork home a lot and does it in his home office."

"Oh!" I squeaked, excitement bubbling up in my belly like fermentation fizz. Paperwork! Home office! *Bingo!*

"Here, I'll show you how to read this gauge, Cat," Greg said.

"Okay!" I bent over beside him and our fingers touched on the rim of the tank. It gave me such a thrill that I jumped a couple of inches. The clothespin popped off my nose and landed in a bucket of green slop. Oops.

Instantly a stench cloud wafted up my nose. My sniffer started to quiver, then my throat. Oh no. If I threw up all over the hoses and tanks, I'd probably ruin the experiment *and* my chances at project partner! Plus, no more spying for V.I.P. passes!

Do not puke, I ordered myself. I had to get to fresh air fast. I squeezed my nostrils shut, super-tight, then said, "Say! I'll start taking notes right now! I've got a pen and notepad in my backpack. I'll run and get them, okay?" I bolted for the door.

"Okeydoke, Cat," Greg murmured, fiddling with a valve.

I ducked out of the garage and hurried into the house, taking in huge gulps of fresh air. Phew! Heading down the hallway, I spied a dark tiny room lined with bookshelves. Omigosh. Mr. T's home office! My heart started to thump thump thump in eagerness.

Right in the middle of the room was a metal desk. "Jackpot," I whispered, rubbing my hands together gleefully. "Mr. T's desk." Inside one of those drawers, there had to be several sheets of pure gold—backstage passes to Woodland Arena!

I yanked open a drawer and tossed papers left and right. I opened another drawer and chucked office supplies over both shoulders.

Suddenly I heard footsteps in the hallway. Eek.

Slowly, I looked over to the door.

There stood Mrs. Twitchell, a laundry basket in her arms. Her eyes bore holes in my head. She stared at the load of papers and business forms in my arms.

"Cat," she said quietly, "what on earth . . ."

Thud. My heart landed on the home-office carpet.

"Oh, um, I can explain, Mrs. Twitchell," I stammered. I dropped the armload of papers on the desktop and mashed them all together, trying to make a quick tidy pile.

Mrs. T looked super-perplexed. She shook her head at me.

I felt my Cat fur begin to rise. Catherine Anne Carlson, incarcerated in juvenile prison for attempted burglary. Headline: PRETEEN CAT BURGLAR CAUGHT RED-PAWED.

A juvie at age eleven. Not good.

"I'm sorry," I peeped. Frantically, I tried to come up with an alibi. My eyes landed on a stack of photograph albums. "Uh," I said feebly, "you see, I have this friend. She really likes Greg. She wishes she had a picture of him to put in her locker at school. And what I was trying to do here was, uh, try to find Greg's photo album, that's all. Like maybe a picture that I could borrow for that friend of mine who likes him . . ."

Mrs. Twitchell's face softened.

"*That friend* who likes Greg?" she said, and winked.

Oh no. Mrs. T thought the crushed girl was me. (Which, in truth, it was . . . but I didn't want her to know that!)

Mrs. Twitchell set down the laundry basket, picked up the stack of albums and gently took my arm. "Oh, Cat," she said. "I do understand. I know my Greg is a darling. I'll never forget when I was a third grader and cut a boy's picture out of the library edition of the school yearbook to keep for myself. Wasn't that terrible? I really do understand, Cat."

Mrs. T led me to the living room and nudged me onto the couch. She grabbed more armloads of photo albums off the bookshelves.

The massive couch sucked me in super-deep. Mrs. T's sizable thighs boxed me in too. I had no hope of escape as she began to exhibit the ceiling-high stack of kiddie photo albums on the coffee table in front of us. Greg's baby pictures, a billion in all.

Mrs. T handed a toddler shot to me. "Isn't that the most

adorable picture of a little boy you've ever seen in your entire life?" she insisted.

"Oh, absolutely." For the first time in days, I wasn't lying. I gazed upon picture after childhood picture and began to wonder how in the world I'd gone through six whole years at Lewis Elementary without noticing that Greg Twitchell was gorgeous.

With his hair off his face, his big blue eyes showed. My gosh, it was enough to make me wilt. I was positive none of the other girls knew what they were missing.

Mrs. T gently tapped the edge of Greg's kindergarten picture and said quietly, "I've pleaded with Greg to go to the barber and get his hair cut short again. He refuses, which is such a mystery to me. He's the perfect son and we only have tiffs over one thing—his hair. Sometimes I think he's hiding behind it. But from what? I've asked him and he won't tell me."

"I don't know, Mrs. Twitchell," I murmured, feasting my eyes on more too-cute pictures.

Just then Greg stuck his head into the living room. With his furry fringe covering his eyes, I couldn't tell where he was looking exactly, but I know for sure he saw the album in my hand. His mouth fell open and he began to blush like crazy.

Oh no! I thought frantically. This is *too* embarrassing! Greg probably thinks I arranged this whole rendezvous at his house so I could get my Cat paws on his baby pictures!

My own face blasted off the blush-o-meter. I rocketed off the Twitchells' couch.

"Oh!" said Mrs. T. "Can't you stay a little longer, Cat? I'd love to show you Greg's baby clothes. I saved a whole box of them."

"Gosh, Mrs. Twitchell," I said, withering, "I've really got to go now. Homework, dinner, all that jazz . . ." I bolted toward the front door, but my jumbo boot toe caught the leg of a chair. I tripped, catapulted forward and banged *smack* into the living room wall. I saw a whole constellation of pretty twinkling stars for about ten seconds.

I turned around woozily and wondered where my glasses had flown off to. Mrs. T picked them up off the carpet and handed them to me. "Are you all right, dear?" she asked.

I nodded and put my glasses back on but things still looked fuzzy. I knew all the smudges on the lenses weren't to blame. I'd knocked myself bonkers . . . so much so that I forgot at that moment to consider Greg's feelings entirely. Suddenly the pressing question popped back into my head and it tumbled off my tongue: "By any chance, does Mr. Twitchell, as Woodland Arena manager, get V.I.P. passes . . . several of which he might generously offer to a certain deserving V.I.P.—Very Important Preteen?"

Mrs. T looked surprised. "Mr. Twitchell never handles backstage passes, dear," she replied. "The events manager might, but not the food service manager."

Huh? Food service? Mr. T didn't manage red-hot pop stars. He managed . . . *hot dogs and popcorn*?

Suddenly Greg shook his shaggy head. His mouth tightened into a straight line. Then he stomped past me and out the front door.

Oh no! Things had gone from bad to worse! I grabbed my backpack off the chair and cried, "Thanks for the lemonade, Mrs. Twitchell. I have to go now, bye!" I flew out the door and clomped fast up the street until I caught up with Greg.

"Greg! Please wait. I can explain," I pleaded. "Please?"

He stopped walking and crossed his arms over his chest. "I never thought you'd be like all the other girls," he muttered. "What is it with that Milo guy, anyhow?"

"Look, Greg. I don't care if I'm within a million miles of Milo Lennox," I lied. I would absolutely *love* to see Milo perform "Cute Little Nerdgirl" live, but I sure couldn't tell Greg that! Eeerrgghh. I hated lying to a boy this nice. I had to tell Greg at least part of the truth. Suddenly I jabbered on about how much I needed a girlfriend at Lewis Elementary with Annie gone in France . . . how Shana kept hogging Cassidy . . . how Shana had decided I was the reigning queen of Loserdom . . .

"You see, Greg," I said quietly, "scoring Shana an early-bird audition is my only hope of ever getting on her good side. I'm really sorry. The last thing I wanted to do was make you feel used."

Greg didn't say anything. I wished I could brush his hair off his forehead. It was hard telling how mad a person was when you couldn't see his eyes.

Eventually I sighed. "Well, good-bye, Greg." My bony

shoulders falling into a slump, I turned and walked up the street.

Now I'd definitely blown it. I'd lost Greg as a friend. And if I didn't follow through on my promise to Shana, I'd lose Cassidy, too.

13

Hotel Sleuthhound

"**C**at!" Lizzie yelled from down the hall. It was seven-thirty Tuesday night. I was sitting at my desk, writing out my spelling words three times each and listening to "Cute Little Nerdgirl" on the Walkman again. Every time I heard this song, I loved it more! It just made me want to twirl through a room on my tip-toes.

"Cat!" Lizzie yelled again.

I yanked off the headphones.

"The phone is for you," Lizzie hollered, "and it's a *boy*!"

A *boy*? I dropped my pen and jumped out of my desk chair. No boy had ever called me before.

I ran and grabbed the phone from Lizzie. She was giggling her head off. "Shhh, Lizzie," I hissed. "Stop it!"

She clamped her hand over her mouth and sat on the top step to listen in.

"Hello?" I said warily into the receiver.

"Cat? This is Greg."

"Greg! Hi!"

Lizzie laughed like a loon and squealed, "Puppy love for Cat!"

"Knock it off, Lizzie!" I barked, and shooed her away. Still giggling, she returned to her room and shut the door. Then I said into the phone, "Sorry about my sister . . . and the whole V.I.P. pass thing. . . ."

"That's all right, Cat. I understand. Making friends at our school can be harder than getting straight A's. Anyhow, I really need your help on the science project."

Oh! Relief flooded my arteries. I hadn't lost Greg as a friend!

"That's great," I replied. "I'll take super-thorough notes. I can cut up the cabbage and stir the goop and tighten bolts on the scooter or whatever you need. I know you'll win—"

"*We'll* win, Cat," Greg said firmly. "And in exchange for all your help, I'd like to help you get that tryout for Shana . . . if that's what you actually want."

"Really?" I squeaked.

"Yes. But this has to be top secret, so I don't get my dad in trouble. I made some calls and this is what I found out. Backstage passes are almost impossible to get for kids. But the head of security at the arena is a good friend of our family's, and he gave me information that's even better."

"What?" My stomach did a double backflip.

"The name of the hotel where Milo is staying in Minneapolis. Shana could show Milo her dance steps there, hours before the actual contest—"

"Greg!" I breathed. "That's a great idea!"

"Please don't tell anybody I told you this," he whispered.

"I won't! I promise."

"Do you have a pen and paper?"

"Just a second." I ran and grabbed a gel pen and notepad off my desk, then scrambled back to the phone. I scribbled like mad as Greg told me, in super-hushed tones, Milo's itinerary.

"The tour buses arrive from Chicago at about five-thirty this Sunday morning," Greg whispered. "The band is staying, just one night, at the Hotel Saint Anthony in downtown Minneapolis. A limousine will arrive at the hotel at seven A.M. to take the band to a breakfast meeting at some fancy restaurant. From there, the limousine will take them to their sound check at Woodland Arena. That's it, Cat. I hope this helps."

"Oh yes, Greg. Thanks!"

"No problem. I've got to go now. I just saw a squirrel run into the garage. I can't let the neighborhood rodents eat the rutabagas!"

I hung up the telephone and danced in my platform boots.

This was beyond awesome! I couldn't wait to tell Cassidy and Shana!

Hold on a second. We needed a ride to the hotel Sunday morning. If I found us a driver, Shana would be doubly grateful to me.

I clomped downstairs and found Mom in the dining room, grading papers. I told her all about the plan and begged for a ride.

"I'm afraid not, Cat," Mom replied.

"But whyyyyy, Mom?"

"You know that kind of music gives me hives." Mom scratched her stomach.

"But you don't have to hear a single itty-bitty note," I insisted. "You only need to drop us off and wait in the car while we meet Milo."

Mom breathed deeply and drummed her fingers on her grade book. "I really don't want to spend Sunday morning stalking a celebrity, Cat."

"Stalking? Who's stalking?"

"Besides," Mom added, "somebody has to stay home and clean this filthy house." She smiled annoyingly, then bent her head back over her grade book.

I *tsk*ed and huffed. My gosh, I couldn't wait to get my own driver's license!

I grabbed the telephone and rang up Shana. I knew her dad was a sure set of wheels to the Hotel Saint Anthony. He always said yes to Shana.

She answered the phone and I cried, "Guess what! I found out which hotel Milo is staying in when he comes to town! The Hotel Saint Anthony in downtown Minneapolis! You can audition there on Sunday, when the tour buses arrive at five-thirty. That's hours before the contest. You'll be the first dancer Milo sees!"

Shana screamed so loudly over the phone, my ear throbbed. The second she stopped shrieking, I said, "But my mom can't drive us."

"I'll get a ride with my dad," Shana replied.

Huh? Didn't she mean *we'll* get a ride with him?

"All Dad does on Sunday mornings is read the sports pages anyhow," Shana babbled excitedly. "Gotta go, Cat." And she hung up on me.

I heard the *click* and dial tone. I stared at the receiver and my blood started to simmer. No "thank you"? No "can't wait for the three of us to do this super-fun thing together—since *you* scored the inside scoop, Cat"?

I was getting ditched again. I just knew Shana would invite Cassidy along to the hotel and leave me in the dust. Well, I wasn't going to miss out on *both* the concert and the hotel!

I snatched the phone again, quickly called Cassidy and told her about the hotel scoop (except the fact that Greg was the supersleuth. That was a secret I'd keep forever).

The second Cassidy stopped screaming over the line, I begged, "But I really want to go, Cassidy. Could you ask Shana? She listens to you."

"Of course! I'll call you right back."

I hated asking Cassidy to do the slimy work, but I just couldn't risk standing up to Shana. I knew if I took her on, she'd boot me so far out of the group that I'd wind up on another continent.

Cassidy rang me back a couple of minutes later with great news. The three of us were going to the Hotel Saint Anthony Sunday morning!

"Woo-hoo!" I cried. I couldn't *wait* to do something this fun with Cassidy!

"We get to see that hot popster's tour bus!" Cassidy shrieked.

And here was my chance to tell Milo how much I liked "Cute Little Nerdgirl."

* * *

Wednesday morning before first bell, Shana grumbled, "Okay, you can come. But if you *trip* me during my audition, Klutzilla—"

"I'll stay out of your way, Shana," I promised, like the coward she'd turned me into.

"You better!" She danced into 6A and I gulped. If I bit my tongue much longer, I'd bite it right off!

* * *

At lunchtime that Wednesday, Shana wolfed her energy bar and gulped her milk, then dashed out to the playground to polish her routine. Fabulous! Five minutes alone with Cassidy!

"What do you think I should wear to the hotel, Cassidy?" I

asked, munching my tuna sandwich and peering under the table at my tiger-stripe pants. I'd tripped so many times in my mastodon heels lately that the hole in the leg was twice as big now. I couldn't wear torn pants to meet a world-famous pop star!

Cassidy didn't answer. I looked up. She was chomping an apple and gazing at Greg. He was peering into the cafeteria trash can, probably searching for more recyclables to use in lab experiments.

"Boy," Cassidy said through a mouthful of apple, "one look at Greg's moptop and I just want to grab a pair of scissors and cut cut cut. Oh, I love mega-makeovers! That would be *so* fun!"

"He'd never go for that," I said. "He's had that sheepdog look since first grade. *Shhh.* Here he comes."

Greg was shuffling in his loafers past our table when suddenly Cassidy reached out and gently took his arm. "Guess what, Greg," she said quietly. "I'm a professional hairdresser practically and you know, if you'd ever like—"

That same second, Judd the Jerk shot out of nowhere. I swear, that creep lurked in the shadows, waiting to pick on Greg at every opportunity. He dived close to Greg's ear and hissed, loudly enough that I heard too, *"Twitchell's got baby-blue eyes."* Judd ran off laughing and Greg turned bright red. Greg stomped off and disappeared out the cafeteria doors.

Omigosh. How long had Judd the Jerk teased Greg about his sapphire gems? Since first grade, I bet. Well, that explained the shaggy-dog bangs.

Back at the lockers after lunch, I cornered Greg and whispered, "Why don't you stand up to Judd, Greg?"

"I'm considering it," Greg whispered back. "And how about you? Will you stand up to Shana? She's always putting you down."

Hmm. Greg had noticed too. "Someday I just might, Greg," I whispered thoughtfully.

✳ ✳ ✳

During art that afternoon, Cassidy and Shana jabbered on and on about the finishing touches on Shana's diva getup—the audition eye shadow . . . the audition nail polish . . .

"I'll do your hair in a French twist, Shana, if you like. It'll take me a while, with your super-long hair, but it'll be *so* worth it!" Cassidy gushed. "A cute twist will help you win that contest, I'm sure of it!"

I sighed. I wanted Cassidy to help *me* with my hotel-rendezvous outfit too. But I just knew Shana would nab every second of Cassidy's time before then. I was on my own at the controls of Style Express. Yikes. The thought made me nibble a fingernail.

At final bell, I whispered to Cassidy, "Could I borrow some copies of *Sizzle Pop* tomorrow?" I was sure there would be pictures of hip-dressing music fans in it. I had to find out what they wore!

"Sure! I'll bring a bunch to school."

And that's how I came to be lugging home a backpack filled with music magazines at three-thirty Thursday. And

✳ ✳

Cassidy had thrown in the September issue of *Lowdown on High Fashion,* too. "I thought you might enjoy looking at the latest styles, Cat," she said sweetly.

✳ ✳ ✳

Thursday night, I put my study skills to work, poring over *Lowdown on High Fashion* like it was a reference book. I memorized all the denim vocabulary words in the article "Cool-Blue Buzzwords," such as *sandblasted, distressed, extreme wash, stonewashed.* . . .

I spied a denim mini on the page, a super-cute distressed skirt with a frayed hem. Boy, I liked it. But yikes, the price? Fifty-five dollars!

I emptied my bank and counted my life savings. $4.27. I couldn't collect my next allowance until Monday and I hadn't dog-walked since Saturday. Drat!

I turned the page. YEE-HAW! COWGIRL CRAZE HOT LOOK FOR FALL! the next headline hollered. I studied the models in suede fringe skirts, rawhide vests, cowboy boots and turquoise jewelry. . . .

"Well," I murmured to myself, "this fad'll make horse freaks Billie and Brooke more popular than ever. But I'm not going to a hoedown! I've got to find out what a girl wears to meet a megastar!"

I chucked *Lowdown on High Fashion* aside and grabbed a copy of *Sizzle Pop.* I studied the photos of fans at concerts. Lots of girls wore minis, and denim was everywhere.

I looked up at my life-size poster of Milo. Even he was

wearing jeans. Hmm. Maybe I could find some cool used jeans at Resurrection Duds. They would probably be ten times cooler than my discount-store pair, which weren't even faded.

Friday after school, I walked alone to Resurrection Duds with my four bucks in my hot paw.

"Half price on all skirts today," Dolores said the second I stepped into the store.

"I'm looking for jeans," I said.

"Try on as many pairs as you like, hon. And I've got jean skirts on that rack over there." Dolores pointed with her super-long red fingernail and cracked her gum.

"Really?" I asked excitedly. "Any minis?"

"I'll help you look, sweetie." Dolores tip-tapped over in her high heels and thumbed through the hangers with her crimson nails. "Here's a comfy old blue-jean skirt, honey. It's regularly six dollars. Only three today, on sale."

"I like that it's stonewashed, but it's long," I said, my heart sinking. "It would come to my knees."

The next second I had a flash of girl genius. "I'll try it on anyhow!" I grabbed the skirt from Dolores, leaped into the dressing room, yanked off my tiger-stripe pants and tugged on the jean skirt.

It fit! I sailed out and modeled for Dolores.

"Too bad it's not a mini," she said. "That would look so cute with your long legs."

"But it can be one," I said excitedly. "Do you have a big pair of scissors?"

"I do, hon." Dolores scurried over to the counter and dug in a drawer.

"Could you cut it off for me?" I asked.

Dolores smiled. "One custom mini, coming right up." And she got busy clipping, very carefully, nearly a foot above my bony kneecaps, cracking her gum like fireworks.

Dolores finished and stepped back. "Oh, that is darling! And it looks dynamite with those platform boots. Do you want me to stitch up the hem for you?"

"Frayed hems are in," I said, suddenly bursting with fashion know-how.

"Well, then, hand it over, hon, and I'll help you fray those edges," Dolores replied with a smile.

And just like that, Dolores had the skirt on top of the counter and was making the hem all fuzzy, picking at it with her ruby fingernail. I wanted to help but I had *zero* nails left after my nervous weeks of consuming them. I made a mental note: Stop chewing nails! Then I could fray hems too. Besides, nice nails would be more stylish than gnawed-off ones. What was a Cat without a decent set of claws, anyhow?

Fifteen minutes later, I was heading home with my customized mini and scrap denim. I hugged the bag happily. "I *can* do this fashion stuff. And on a budget too!" I whispered to myself, and danced inside.

Up in my room, I stuffed the shopping bag deep in my closet. I knew Mom's eyebrows would shoot to Jupiter at the sight of that skirt. And if she knew I was planning on pairing it with Cassidy's yellow tank, she'd really flip. I could just hear her say, "That whole ensemble is weather inappropriate. Now, let's use some common sense." Then she'd make me wear my itchy wool Norwegian sweater on top and my old bumpy, lumpy brown tights on the bottom. It's true, nights were near freezing now in our neck of the woods, but that was beside the point. Mom would ruin my glam look in a millisecond!

I didn't have time for debates. It was time to think about hairdos.

Without Cassidy's hairdresser brain to pick, I studied the pictures in *Sizzle Pop* again. I found a style that I liked on one fan. But I couldn't fix my hair that way today or I'd freak out my family.

Okay, then, I'd set my alarm for super-early Sunday morning and put my plans in motion.

14

Descending the Tour Bus Steps

"**B**e sure to wake me up before you leave in the morning, Cat." Mom kissed me on top of my head.

I pretended to be asleep already and even added a phony snore. I didn't want to lie outright to my mom, but no way would I wake her up in the morning. She'd veto everything about my meet-Milo outfit.

"Good-night, honey." Mom clicked off my light and shut my door.

It took me ages to conk out. I was *so* excited! Finally, I fell asleep . . .

. . . and my alarm blasted me awake at 4 A.M. I leaped out of bed and grabbed the three long skinny strips I'd cut from the scrap denim the night before, then tiptoed to the bathroom.

Bleary-eyed, I yawned hugely at the mirror. I forced my eyelids open with all ten digits, then got busy transforming my extreme bed head.

Fifteen minutes later, I had three spiky ponytails sticking out the top of my head, just like the girl I'd seen in *Sizzle Pop*. I clipped flyaway hairs back with yellow and purple barrettes, then tied a denim ribbon at the base of each spike to match my mini. Cute!

But the spikes were a little droopy, in spite of all those colorful rubber binders. What to do? We'd never had any hair spray in our house, out of respect for the ozone layer.

I quickly dug in our bathroom drawers. Eeerrgh! Mom was such a beauty minimalist that she had *no* mousse or hair gels. So what could give my spikes some holding-up power?

I stole down the hall to the study and grabbed a bottle of white glue. I crept back to the bathroom and mixed a little of it with water in my palm, then rubbed it on my spikes. Perfect! They stuck straight up now, like the quills on a nervous porcupine.

Then I scrubbed the smudges off my glasses and tiptoed back to my room. In no time flat, I had on the yellow tank, the blue-jean mini and my purple platform boots.

I slipped on my glasses and stepped in front of my mirror.

I blinked in surprise. "Helloooo," I whispered to the triple-spiked girl in the torn-edge miniskirt, "have we met before?"

I knew I'd *wow* Cassidy and Shana today. But even better, I was wowing myself. For the first time in eleven years, I felt head-to-toe stylish. This was *fun*.

Only one problem. No accessories. Hmm. I'd seen a girl in *Sizzle Pop* wearing a musical-note bracelet. Yes, I'd try that. . . .

I quickly ripped a two-inch-wide strip off the scrap denim, then tied it around my left wrist, using my teeth and the fingers of my right hand to make a knot. I grabbed a felt-tip pen off my desk and began to draw a musical staff and treble clef on the denim. Slowly and quietly, I hummed the melody of "Cute Little Nerdgirl," then penned the notes on the staff.

Voilà. I held out my arm and admired my fave-tune bracelet. It would definitely show Milo and the rest of the world this fan's connection to his special song. I blew my bracelet a dramatic air kiss, then slipped the pen into my mini pocket. I'd need it to get Milo's autograph!

I tiptoed out my door and managed to creep down the stairs in my jumbo soles without making a sound. Silently, I opened our front door and locked it behind me with the house key I'd borrowed off Mom's key chain. I slipped the key into my boot, then crept down to the street and plopped my butt on the curb. I wanted Mr. Fitz to see me the second the Jeep turned the corner so he wouldn't honk and wake my mom.

Brrrr. My teeth started to chatter. I rubbed my goose bump–covered arms. "Never mind a minor little frosty wind-chill factor," I whispered to myself, shivering like crazy. "The weather is beautiful and so am I."

Finally, the Jeep pulled up. I hopped into the backseat and got to sit right next to Cassidy!

"Hi, Cat," Cassidy squealed. "*Meow*-za, you look *fab*!"

Shana didn't even turn around from the front to say hi. "Let's go, Dad," she said impatiently. "We better be the only girls there, but if we're not, we *have* to be the *first*!"

Mr. Fitz floored it and zoomed down Lucille Street Hill. He had his Viking helmet on, horns and all. He looked in the rearview mirror at me and said sleepily, "Go, Vikes, eh, Cat? Big game yesterday. The Vikes sacked 'em!" He gave a humongous yawn, then smacked his lips.

Cassidy was still staring at me, her pink-glossed mouth hanging open. "I just loooove your frayed mini, blue-jean ribbons and cool spikes, Cat!" she gushed.

"Thanks, Cassidy!" I said, and grinned confidently. I could hardly believe that a fashion triumph moment was actually happening to me!

Shana turned around and gawked at me. I gawked right back. Her sparkly eye shadow, shimmering rouge and glitter hair spray were as twinkly as her rhinestone-covered top and mini. She looked like a jewelry store all lit up for a sidewalk sale.

She growled, "Are you trying to upstage my audition outfit with that hip mini, Cat?"

Holy cow. She'd said *hip*. That was the closest thing to a compliment Dragon Girl had ever spat at me! But my happiness didn't last very long. Shana was still staring at me with her eyes narrowed. She mouthed, "You better not, and you know why," and pointed her finger at Cassidy.

Oh, I wished I had a dirty old sock to stuff in that fat mouth of Shana's, to keep my secret trapped inside!

Cassidy was busy admiring my bracelet. "Did you make that yourself, Cat? Let me see!" She grabbed my arm and said, "This is the sweetest thing I ever saw. What song is it?"

"Cute—" I started to say, but then caught myself. I couldn't tell them that "Cute Little Nerdgirl" was my favorite song. I might as well confess outright that I was a brainiac!

"Actually, it's the notes to 'Goddess Caffeina,' " I lied quickly, holding out my wrist. I sure hoped they couldn't read music.

Shana stared at the denim band for a minute, her eyes dripping suspicion. Finally, she turned back around and barked, "Hurry up, Dad!"

I took a deep breath and tried to relax as the little white Jeep zoomed over the mighty Mississippi toward downtown Minneapolis. Mr. Fitz kept yawning as loudly as a grizzly bear. He sped down Highway 94, his rude morning breath totally fogging up the windshield. The bad-breathed baboon leaned forward to wipe the steamy glass and the Jeep swerved just as a semitrailer came roaring past us.

"Look out, Dad!" Shana yelled. Another semi plowed past us. "Dad, watch it!"

Cassidy grabbed my hand in a death grip and whimpered.

I squeezed her fingers tight and whispered, "Eek! We're

going to get squished!" Luckily we were sitting together so we could hold hands. If Shana and I touched fingers, we'd both probably puke.

"I've got it under control, girls." Mr. Fitz yawned hugely again. His whole whisker-covered face scrunched up, squeezing his eyes shut. The geezer was half-asleep at the wheel!

I was petrified bedrock by the time we pulled into the hotel parking lot. Suddenly Shana shrieked, "Cripes! The tour buses are already here!"

"Go get that there autograph, girls," Mr. Fitz mumbled sleepily. He reached for the Sunday newspaper that lay on the floor of the Jeep and pulled out the sports pages.

Shana scrambled like an egg out of the Jeep, then shot across the asphalt with Cassidy and me trailing five feet behind her. "Come on, guys, hurry!" she called over her shoulder.

"I'm so excited I might pee my pants, Cat!" Cassidy whispered as she ran.

"Me too! Do you think he'll sing for us or play his guitar?" I whispered back, my heart booming along with my big boots.

"I hope both!" Cassidy said.

We dashed around the back of the rear tour bus and stopped dead in our boot tracks. There must've been some big leaks in the top-secret itinerary files along the way. At least two dozen girls were peering in the tinted windows of the tour buses. Ten more were dancing on the sidewalk, screaming, "Watch me, Milo!"

Shana looked panic-stricken. One teenage girl was doing some amazing moves. She wore cool glitter jeans and a neon yellow T-shirt that said:

PICK ME FOR
BACKUP DANCER,
I'M THE BEST!!

"Gosh, that girl is really good," Cassidy murmured.

Oh no, Shana had met her match. If Milo ignored Shana's talent, I was doomed.

"Go, Shana, quick!" I yelled. "You have to show Milo how good you are, right now!"

Shana's eyes filled with competitive fire. She started to dance like a windup toy, hollering, "I'm fantastic, Milo, see?" She boogied all over the sidewalk and bumped a few girls onto the grass.

Cassidy grabbed my arm and hauled me into the crowd. The mob of girls moved in waves between the two tour buses. Everybody stood on tiptoe, trying to catch glimpses of the band through the dark windows.

Then a girl screamed so loudly, I almost leaped out of my mini. The door on the front tour bus was opening! Cameras starting flashing like crazy as everyone surged forward. Cassidy cried, "Yikes! We're gonna get trampled!"

But she and I pushed ahead too, trying to get elbow-rubbing close to Milo. Moments later, all the girls stopped shoving and went, "Ooooh." A big beefy guy with ultra-tattooed arms lumbered down the bus steps.

"The bodyguard," Cassidy breathed.

"Yo," the beefy guy bellowed at the mob. "Now don't any of you try to jump on any stars' bones or I'll have to tie you into taffy."

Now, this was a watchdog. Not like Puff.

Suddenly Jarvis, the band's piano player, stepped out of the bus. Next, Duke, the drummer. Then all the girls started to scream, "Milo! I love you, Milo!" And there he was! Descending the steps, wearing blue jeans and a leather jacket and holding his cool yellow guitar!

A teenage girl burst into tears. "I love you *so* much, Milo!" she blubbered into her hands.

Milo looked fifty times cuter in real life than in his posters. My ticker was practically catapulting out of my rib cage! I'd never seen anybody famous up close before, and nobody this talented. "Milo!" I yelled. "There's one of your songs I really love! It's so special!"

"I'm gonna *die*!" Cassidy cried. "It's really him!"

The crowd squished tighter around Milo, everybody waving pens like swords and screaming, "Milo! Give me your autograph!"

"Pick me to dance tonight, Milo!" the girl in the neon tee shrieked.

I spotted Shana in the crowd. *"I'm better than her, Milo!*

I've practiced for weeks*!"* Shana screamed, her face matching her red mini and top.

Milo, Duke, Jarvis and the bodyguard dived into the entrance of the Hotel Saint Anthony. Suddenly the whole mob of girls shot toward the revolving door in one mushy, pushy mass.

"Cat!" Shana hollered, totally wild-eyed and frantic. "What are we going to do now?"

Gulp. "Follow me!" I yelled, and pulled Shana and Cassidy forward.

One by one, we all found ourselves inside the spinning pie-shaped glass chambers, trying to weasel our way inside. The bodyguard blocked the entrance. Every time one of us tried to pop out of the revolving door into the hotel, he pushed our arms and legs back inside the glass carousel and sent us spinning around again. We were trapped, circling round and round and round. I started to get soooo dizzy.

"I'm gonna barf!" Cassidy yelled. She jumped out the exit. A bunch of other girls toppled out and looked green in the face. Shana and I were left in the glass carousel, still spinning in circles. It was time to get assertive.

When I reached the entrance, I stuck out my head. The bodyguard shoved me back in and tried to start the spin cycle again—but my spikes were caught in the door.

"Yiiiiiihhhh!" I screamed.

15

Preteen
Private Eye

"**S**top your shrieking!" Muttonhead yelled at me through the glass. *"Ya wanna get us all kicked outta this hotel?"*

But I couldn't stop! My hair was caught in the door and it *hurt*!

Walnut Brain finally seemed to grasp the problem. He sent the carousel spinning in the opposite direction and released my spearhead. I tumbled out the exit, one hand on my stinging scalp, the other on my queasy stomach. Woozily, I made a crooked beeline for the boulevard, where I crumpled into a nauseated lump next to Cassidy on the little patch of perfect grass.

Shana came marching out of the revolving door. "Now what?" she demanded, her hands on her hips.

I thought hard for four seconds, then said, "Okay. This is what we do. We walk casually back to the Jeep and pretend we're leaving. Then we sneak back in as soon as the bodyguard is gone from the door."

Cassidy rubbed her hands together and giggled. "This is so fun," she said. "We'll get Milo's autograph yet."

"*And* an early tryout, Shana. Don't worry," I said firmly, and gulped. Then I led the way across the lot to the Jeep.

Mr. Fitz was in the front seat with his head back and the sports pages draped over his face. He was snoring so hard, the paper was rattling and quivering with every honking exhale.

"Excellent," Shana whispered. "He sleeps like a rock. We have hours to hunt for Milo before Dad wakes up!"

We hunkered down behind the car and peered around the front wheel at the hotel. The girl in the neon tee was squatting behind a giant clay pot filled with geraniums. More girls were hidden in bushes beside the entrance and Muttonhead's massive body was still blocking it.

I had to get Shana inside the hotel before the competition!

"Okay, guys," I whispered, "we're going inside and finding Milo in this big hotel right now."

"How?" Cassidy asked, and giggled quietly.

I had no idea. "I've got a goof-proof plan," I lied, and was thisclose to moaning out loud . . . when I spied a side door!

"Come on, guys, follow me," I whispered. "Stay low, out of sight."

We crept across the parking lot on our hands and knees

behind parked cars until we reached the door. A sign on it said DELIVERIES. I yanked on the handle—and it opened!

We breezed right in, tiptoed down a long corridor and hid behind a tall plant. Wide-eyed, I gawked at the hotel lobby. "Holy cow." There were crystal chandeliers and bellhops hopping all over the place.

"Look at the velvet chairs," Cassidy breathed. "Wow, this is a fancy joint."

"No kidding," I whispered.

"Who cares?" Shana said snottily. "Let's just find Milo."

Gosh, I wished she'd relax. Cassidy and I would be having fifty times more fun if we could just ditch grand-champ grump Miss Fitz!

"We have to sneak through the lobby somehow," I whispered. "The bodyguard is still by the front door. At least his back is turned to us." I peered over Shana's high-wattage rhinestone shoulder and spied the elevator doors across the lobby. They were standing wide open. "Hurry," I whispered, "but don't make a noise."

We tiptoed past the front desk. One hotel clerk had her nose to a computer screen, busy making a reservation. The other was gabbing on a telephone. They didn't even look up as we pussyfooted past.

I moved slowly and carefully across the fancy-schmancy carpet. I was still so unsteady in my towering heels, and Shana's threatening words still rang loudly in my ears: "Don't *trip* me at my audition, Klutzilla, or else!" If I fell over a fancy statue—or, worst of all, Shana herself!—I'd ruin everything. I couldn't mess up Shana's morning even a microscopic bit or I'd earn myself instant *non*membership in this clique.

We darted unseen into the open elevator and squeezed against the side wall so the bodyguard couldn't see us if he turned around. Cassidy giggled nervously.

I was standing next to the button control panel. "Celebrities stay in penthouse suites, don't they?" I whispered.

"They do in the movies," Cassidy whispered back.

"So let's go already, Cat," Shana hissed. She reached around me and gave 15, the top-floor button, a jab.

The door didn't move. I gave the button another poke.

The door still didn't budge a millimeter! "Come on, close," I pleaded with it in a whisper. Just then a wrinkly old man in a lavender golf shirt stepped inside the elevator. He was 80 percent bald, with gray hairs combed up and over a substantial pink spot.

He took one look at Shana's rhinestone flashery and his gray unibrow shot sky-high. Yikes, could her diva outfit call any more attention to us? I wished I had a sheet to throw over her head!

Mr. Golf Shirt took a plastic card out of his wallet. He swiped it through a little box attached to the button panel and pressed the ninth-floor button. Suddenly the elevator door closed. We started to go up. Oh, so that was the trick! We needed an ID card to operate this contraption.

I quickly gave the top-floor button a jab.

"Shouldn't you be with your parents?" he said, wiggling his unibrow at me. Eek. I couldn't get busted and booted out of this hotel before Shana had a chance to audition!

"Absolutely. We're on our way to meet them now," I replied with my most polite smile.

He gave a satisfied nod and got off on the ninth floor. Phew. We whizzed up to the fifteenth, stepped out and looked around. My heart started to go thumpa, thumpa.

"Milo, here we come!" I whispered excitedly.

"Oh yeah? Where are all the penthouse suites?" Shana snorted. "There're hardly any doors up here!"

"This floor does seem a little weird, Cat," Cassidy said, rubbing her chin.

Hmm. Big stacks of portable chairs and two scratched-up wooden tables were shoved against the walls. A rolled-up rug lay in the middle of the hallway floor. Maybe Cassidy was right. This whole floor seemed to be . . . storage.

"I'm sure this look is just a cover," I replied quietly. "You know—to keep fans from the celebrities. I bet behind one of those three doors is a luxurious penthouse suite where Milo is putting his cute feet up right now. Follow me."

I, Cat Carlson, plainclothes girl, preteen private eye, tiptoed down the hall to begin my major sleuthkid moves. Operation: Find Pop Star Dazzler and Make Him Watch Dazzling Dance Routine.

Cassidy giggled quietly.

"Cat, what are you doing?" Shana demanded.

"Conducting espionage," I whispered. "Code name C-A-T." I stopped. "Shhh. I hear something. Do you hear it?"

Cassidy put her hand behind her ear.

I put mine up to a door. "I swear I heard a piano chord," I whispered.

"Excuse me, FBI," Shana drawled. "I have a sug*ges*tion." She pointed at something above my head.

I looked up. LINEN, a little sign painted on the door said.

"I guess the band isn't jamming behind that door," I murmured. "Never mind."

Shana tsked. "Speed it up, Cat. I've got to get to Milo *now*."

Sheesh, why did I have to pick this week to give up nail biting? Shana was making me so nervous!

I tiptoed to the next door. Hmm. A tiny sign there said STORAGE. Only three doors on the entire top floor . . . This was just so odd.

Well then, the third door, down at the end of the hall, had to be the penthouse suite! I felt a surge of excitement being this hot on the cute crooner's trail. To heck with tiptoe-age, I thought, and tromped down the long hallway.

Shana chased along after me, then stopped suddenly and yelled, "Sherlock! Will you *puh*-leeeez get a clue?"

The door said FIRE ESCAPE. I scratched my cheek and said, "Well, this confirms my initial suspicions. This floor is not for hotel guests."

"Cat!" Shana screeched. Her face started to turn purple.

"Be careful, Shana," Cassidy said in a soothing voice, "your face is as purple as your eye shadow. You might bust an artery or something."

"That's not *all* I'm gonna bust!" Shana yelled, looking at my head. She leaped over and rattled the knob on the fire escape door. "It's locked, Cat!" she cried. "It probably opens only if there's a real fire, so the only way down is the elevator. But we can't go down because we don't have an ID card! *Oh no!*" she shrieked. *"We're trapped up here!"*

Oh yes. Oops.

"How can I audition if I can't get to Milo?" Shana grabbed my spaghetti straps and started to yank them to and fro. My head bobbed so hard, it almost snapped off my neck.

Cassidy was staring wide-eyed at the two of us.

I was *thisclose* to hollering at Shana to get her grubs off me when suddenly the elevator opened. A big canvas bin on wheels came rolling out of the elevator door. A little woman wearing a pink maid's uniform pushed the giant basket from behind.

I pulled my spaghetti straps free from Shana's iron grip and dived under one of the old wooden tables. Cassidy scrambled in beside me and grabbed my hand.

Shana backed up against a wall.

"Come hide under here, Shana," I whispered. "Quick! If you get caught, we'll all get thrown out of the hotel!"

But she was frozen solid, like a big chunk of ice in the bottom of a soda glass.

Luckily, the little maid rolled the huge basket down the

corridor without seeing Shana and stopped in front of the door marked LINEN. She took a key ring off her pink belt, unlocked the door and disappeared inside.

In a flash, Shana hopped over to the laundry basket and climbed inside. She burrowed deep in the bin filled with used linen. Oh, I got my wish! A sheet to throw over Shana! And even better—a whole pile of gross, dirty ones!

"Shana," Cassidy whispered, "what are you doing?"

"It's my only hope of escape," Shana whispered back.

Cassidy clamped her hand over her mouth. She started to shake with giggles.

Her laughter was contagious. A big guffaw burst out of my mouth.

Just then the maid stepped out of the linen room, carrying a couple of big canvas bags. She looked down at Cassidy and me in surprise. "What are you girls doing here?" she asked, dropping the bags in the laundry basket, on top of Shana's dirty-sheet-covered head.

I had to think fast. "Um—we accidentally got off on the wrong floor."

"Well, that's what the elevator's for," she replied with a shrug, and gave the huge basket a mighty shove into the elevator. Cassidy and I scurried after her. She pressed the basement button and the elevator started to move.

Cassidy began to laugh even more maniacally than before. "Oh oh oh!" she cried, holding her stomach, "so you don't need an ID card to make the elevator go down. Only up!"

The maid stared at Cassidy and shook her head. "Kids today."

I bent over and pretended to rezip my platform boot, putting my nose up close to the canvas basket. "Shana," I whispered, "you can come out now. Did you hear? We don't need an ID card to go *down*."

I straightened back up. Now the maid was staring at *me* like I was loony.

Shana didn't budge. She probably didn't want to scare the maid silly, jumping out like a jack-in-the-box. For once, I agreed with Shana. Making someone die of fright would get us kicked out of this hotel for sure.

Finally, the elevator stopped at the basement and the doors opened.

"Ur-oooomph!" The maid gave a Herculean heave-ho and shoved the basket toward a door that said HOTEL KITCHEN. I jumped forward. "I'm sorry, you can't come in here," the maid said. "Employees only, dear. You and your friend need to go back to the lobby or your room now. Bye."

Cassidy and I looked at each other wildly. "Maybe Shana is suffocating under those foul dirty towels and sheets," I whispered. "We have to get her out and upstairs to Milo!"

Cassidy nodded and gulped as the maid pushed the basket into the kitchen.

Without making a sound, I tiptoed over and opened the swinging door a crack. The smell of frying bacon wafted up my snout. I put my ear up to the door and heard the chop chop chop of kitchen knives on cutting boards.

"Howdy, Bernice," a man called. "Got a pile of dirty towels and aprons here. Didn't have a chance to bag them up. We're short-staffed. Both Wade and Sandy were no-shows today. Stomach flu. We're in trouble, losing two of our room-service gofers on the same morning."

"That's too bad, Sam. I'll get the dirty towels."

I heard Bernice shuffle across the kitchen as Sam grumbled on. "Some band named Milo Something or Other just checked in and ordered coffee. I called Roy and Cedric to get their butts in for some overtime, but it'll take them at least an hour to get here, and we need help with room service runs right *now*."

Hey hey hey, I thought, my eyes bugging out. Here's Opportunity, banging on our door!

I grabbed Cassidy's arm and quietly pulled her into the hotel kitchen. We squeezed into a corner by the deep freeze and peeked into the giant room.

Sam and about twelve other cooks had their backs to us, working away at rows of industrial-size sinks and stoves and cutting boards. Bernice was bent over in the far corner of the mammoth kitchen, picking a heap of used linen off the floor.

Like a cougar, I crept over to the laundry basket and knelt beside it. "Shana," I whispered through the canvas, "come out right now or *no* audition!"

In an instant, Shana was out of the bin and standing next to me. She straightened her rhinestone getup and whipped the long flyaway wisps that had come loose from her French twist away from her face. Cassidy quickly scooted over and joined us.

I mouthed to her and Shana, "I'll handle this." Then I called to the head cook, "Um, hello! Is Wade here? He's our uncle. We're supposed to write school papers on hotel service. Um, Uncle Wade told us that the best way for us to learn about gofer runs is to help out."

Sam peeled his eyes off his soup pot and looked over at us. "Wade's sick today," Sam said. "He didn't tell you girls that?"

"No, sir," I squeaked.

The head chef gawked at Shana's supernova outfit. "What's with all the fake jewels?" he asked.

Eek. I stepped in front of Shana and replied, "We weren't exactly sure what room-service gofers wore."

Sam snorted and said, "Ours wear vests and bow ties. Which you need to get on if you're going to help." He started to wave his giant metal spoon all over the place. "Vests, over there. Bow ties, over there. Whip them on! Hurry up! Go go go!"

On the Hottie's Tin Roof

"**B**ring me that tray of sticky buns, kid," Sam barked at me. "That's something for your school paper. Guests in presidential suites get complimentary rolls when they order gourmet java. You"—he barked at Shana—"grab that carafe and bring it here, on the double!"

Yippee! The three of us dived into action, trying not to choke from the tight bow ties at our necks. We helped Sam get the sweet rolls onto a fancy plate, fill a silver pitcher with cream and stick a sweetheart rose in a vase. Sam filled a pot with coffee, and then we set everything on a shiny silver tray along with fancy napkins and snazzy Hotel Saint Anthony mugs.

"Okay, listen up," Sam said. "If your young uncle Wade can handle gofer runs on his own, the three of you can do it together. Take this tray up the kitchen elevator, over there." Sam jerked his neck at an old elevator in the corner. "Deliver the tray to room 1427 and give it to that band. Do you think you can handle that?"

Oh my *gosh,* could we! My jaw dropped on the industrial linoleum.

Shana gave a yelp and grabbed the tray.

"Hey," Sam snarled. "Careful! Now get going before that java gets cold."

Super-wide-eyed, the three of us headed to the service elevator. "I feel like Goddess Caffeina," Cassidy whispered breathlessly, "delivering Milo his morning coffee!"

"Me too!" I whispered, excitement burbling inside me like a coffeemaker.

The second the door shut behind us and the elevator started to move up, Shana said bossily, "Here, take this, Cat." She shoved the tray into my hands. Then she yanked off her bow tie and hotel vest, chucked them in the corner and started to dance like crazy.

Cassidy eyed the sticky buns. "I sure am hungry," she said, starting to drool.

"I'm starving too," I murmured. Just looking at the thick layer of creamy sugar on top of the rolls made me salivate like a Saint Bernard. "I didn't have any breakfast."

"Me neither." Cassidy's wiggling nostrils moved closer to

the plate of sweet rolls. "Milo wouldn't mind if we borrowed just *one* little bun, would he?" she peeped.

"I don't think so," I said. "We could split one, Cassidy. Besides, I know the band is going out to breakfast—"

"How can you guys even *think* about food now?" Shana said snottily, and began to bop even more feverishly inside the moving elevator. She put her hip-swivel muscles into top gear and began to do some sky-touching kicks. "It's time for me to *ace* this audition and get this gig!"

Hands on her hips, suddenly she did a super-high kick with her right leg. The heel of her glittery dance shoe caught the corner of the tray in my hands. The tray went flying out of my fingers and *crash!* everything landed on the elevator carpet. The lid stayed closed on the coffeepot, but the cream sloshed out of the little pitcher and splashed everywhere.

The sticky buns flew off the plate, sailed up, up, up—and stuck to the ceiling.

Cassidy gasped. Shana went right on dancing.

"We've got to get those buns down from there or we'll be in big trouble," I said.

No response from Shana. I turned around. The elevator doors were open. "Shana?" I said.

She was gone! Cassidy and I stuck our heads out the elevator door and spied her running down the fourteenth floor.

"Shana!" I cried. "Come back here! You can't show up at Milo's door without his morning coffee!"

"Yeah!" Cassidy called. "Wait up!"

Shana ignored us. She dashed to the end of the hallway and disappeared around the corner, bound for room 1427.

Cassidy and I frantically gathered everything off the floor (except the puddles of cream oozing into the carpet) and slapped it all back on the tray. Then we jumped up and down, trying to reach the sticky buns on the ceiling. I managed to nab two rolls and had jumped up to grab another when suddenly . . .

. . . the bodyguard reached into the elevator and grabbed me.

"Hey, let go!" I yelled. I tried to kick his beefy shins but he stuck me under his arm like I was some two-by-four plank.

Bonehead grabbed Cassidy and stuck her under his other brawny arm, where Shana was dangling and hollering, "Get your slimy tentacles off me or I'll call the cops!"

He totally ignored her and hauled us out of the service elevator.

"Cat!" Shana screeched. "*Do* something!"

"Here." I handed her a sticky bun. "Want one?"

"I don't want a sticky bun!" Shana hollered. "I want to *dance* with the *School Glue* tour *tonight*!" she said through her teeth, her face totally scarlet now.

My stomach started to do a twittery jitterbug as I remembered our deal.

"Put us down!" I demanded.

Muttonhead gave a snort. He hauled us to the main hotel elevator and punched the Down button with his kneecap.

Shana squirmed like crazy, trying to wiggle herself free. "I have to see Milo Lennox," she said. "You didn't even let me near his room!"

Beefhead snorted again. The elevator door opened and he kept a bicep-hold on us until we reached the ground floor. Then he hauled us across the hotel lobby, kicked open the delivery door and dumped us onto a little patch of grass by the parking lot. He made Cassidy and me hand over the vests and bow ties. Then he barked, "Now, stay outta this hotel. If you come back in, I'll braid the three of you into a girly ribbon."

He lumbered back into the hotel and disappeared.

That exact second, a white limousine pulled into the hotel parking lot.

"Shana, *look*," I breathed. "It's coming to take the band to breakfast and their sound check. This is another chance for you! You can audition right here, in the parking lot—when Milo comes out of the hotel!"

Shana's eyes started to spin like Ferris wheels in hyperdrive. She jumped to her feet and started to rev up her dance muscles for the third time that morning.

"Hold it," I said. "We have to stay out of sight until the band shows up, or the chauffeur might kick us off the property. Come on, you guys!"

We jumped behind the giant clay pots. Cassidy started to giggle nervously again.

From our hideout, I could see Mr. Fitz in the Jeep. The newspaper was still draped over his hairy head. He was sawing up another big pile of logs.

The mile-long luxury mobile stopped at the hotel's front doors. A chubby chauffeur in a black suit and tie stepped out of the driver's door. He was talking on a cell phone. With his free hand, he gave the windshield a wipe with a white hankie; then he waddled to the back passenger door and opened it. He dropped the phone in his pocket, then stood beside the open back door, straight and still, like a roly-poly statue.

Just then I heard some rustling and faint giggles in the bushes next to us. We looked over and spied half a dozen girls hunkered down, gawking at the limousine through the bushes.

"Oh no," Shana moaned in a whisper, "there's the girl in the neon tee."

I forced myself to stay calm and said evenly, "Don't panic, Shana. This is what we do. The second Milo gets in that limo, you run out and do your dance routine, right next to his window, okay? Cassidy and I will handle the competition."

Shana nodded, but I could see the muscles in her neck and jaw get tighter and tighter while we waited for the band to show up. About ten eternal minutes later, Jarvis, the bodyguard and *Milo* ducked out of the hotel's side door! They scrambled across the sidewalk and dived into the limousine. Chauffeur Chubbins quickly shut the back door behind the band. He stood by the limo, waiting for Duke to come out of the hotel.

Instantly, the pack of girls came screaming out of the bushes and swarmed around the limousine. They pressed their noses against the tinted windows, trying to see inside.

"Go, Shana, quick!" I cried.

She bolted across the sidewalk and started to bop beside the limo. The girl in the neon T-shirt began to boogie right beside her. They both screamed, "Pick me to dance tonight, Milo!"

Then a girl in a tie-dyed tank top leaped over to the limo and hollered, "No, Milo, I'm the best, see?" And she started to rip up the asphalt.

Hmm. How could Cassidy and I get the limelight completely on Shana?

That second, Duke came running out of the hotel, waving a pair of drumsticks in the air. "Got my lucky sticks!" he said as the limo door flew open. In that instant, I spied Milo's curly-haired head and beautiful smile. Oh my gosh! Here was my chance to tell him how much I liked "Cute Little Nerdgirl."

Just then Duke pulled the back door shut and Chauffeur Chubbins waddled to the driver's seat. Luckily, the sunroof was open. If I called loudly, surely Milo would hear me.

"Milo!" I yelled. "Don't go yet! Wait! I want to talk to you for two little seconds!"

I jumped toward the limo at mach speed, totally forgetting to be careful on my tipsy clodhoppers. *Oops.* I tripped over Neon Girl's ankle and went shooting through the air . . .

. . . and plowed right into Shana.

Bowling Pin Fitz went flying and landed on the grass.

Quadruple oops.

Shana shot up like an erupting volcano and started to screech in my face, "You *tripped* me during the audition of a lifetime, Cat Carlson!"

Chauffeur Chubbins revved the engine. . . . Panic filled Shana's eyes. Milo was leaving!

She shouted at me, "What good does your A-plus do me now, Cat? Nothing! I should never have trusted a brainiac geek like you to land me a gig. I knew a nerd couldn't get me up close to a megastar!"

Oh *no*! I glanced over at Cassidy. Her mouth was hanging open, as wide as the Grand Canyon!

My blood started to boil. How *could* Shana blab this stuff in front of Cassidy?

Suddenly my secret was out—and so were my claws. I'd had enough. It was Catfight time!

"Shana Fitz!" I hollered. "I am *so* sick of you calling me names and putting me down! Now, watch this. Even a *nerd* can get a star's attention! I'm going to have a talk with Milo Lennox and it's *not* to beg for an audition for *you*!"

I whirled around and leaped at the luxurious hot rod. I pounced in purrrrrfect Cat fashion, landing on the wide flat trunk.

"Cat!" Cassidy screamed. "What are you doing?"

There was no time for Q and A. I pushed hard off my mountainous soles. With one nimble, tabby-like pounce, I was on top of the ornate crate. I scrambled toward the open sunroof. I'd just poke my head inside and have a quick little chat with Milo about my favorite song.

My hefty heels went thunk thunk thunk on the hottie's tin roof as I scurried closer. I gave another push with my colossal boot toe, but oops . . .

. . . I overshot the mark, slid forward on the belly of my blue-jean mini . . .

. . . and fell headfirst through the sunroof. I managed to perform a decent half gainer in my descent and landed with a thud . . .

. . . directly on Milo's lap.

My nose was one inch from his ultra-handsome, world-famous face . . . only millimeters from the mega-talented, big-hearted boy who wrote "Cute Little Nerdgirl."

I slapped my hand over my mouth, then started to scream.

17

So Long, Babycakes

"**S**towaway!" the bodyguard hollered. He threw open a little sliding window behind the chauffeur's head and barked, "Call hotel security, Tim!"

Then Muttonhead lunged at me.

I grabbed Milo's leather jacket and held on tight. "Wait!" I cried. "I just *have* to tell you how much I love 'Cute Little Nerdgirl,' Milo! That song is pure sunshine for me. It brightens my cloudiest days!"

Milo stared at me.

My limbs turned to mush.

Beefhead grabbed my wrist, right at my musical-note bracelet.

"Don't!" I said. "You'll tear it." I looked at Milo and added, "These are the notes to 'Nerdgirl.'"

Milo held up his hand. "Let go of the kid, Henrick," he said quietly.

Ohhhh, the hot star's golden voice was melting me!

Henrick dropped my wrist and backed off.

Milo gently nudged me off his lap and I scooted onto the seat next to him. "That's why you took a flying leap through the sunroof?" he asked. "To tell me you like that tune?"

I nodded wildly. "Yes!" I quickly dug the felt-tip pen out of my mini pocket. "Would you autograph my bracelet?"

Milo took the pen and scribbled his name below the notes. I gasped and admired his signature. Then I rattled, "It's as if you had X-ray vision into my soul when you wrote this song, Milo. I just know you wrote it for a girl like me!"

Milo studied me, then smiled. "No," he said, "I didn't write that tune for a girl like you."

Huh?

"I wrote that number for a nerd," he said, and winked.

"But," I piped up, "I *am* a nerd."

"If you say so."

I wrinkled my nose, feeling kind of confused. "Well, *I* don't say so, I guess. The kids at my school do."

"Okay. If you want to believe them . . ." He shrugged.

Then he winked again, smiled cutely and said, "So long, babycakes."

Milo gave the nod to Henrick.

And I went *"Wooh!"* because Beefhead yanked me off the seat just as the back door of the limo opened. He handed me over to the hotel security guard and the next thing I knew, I was being led past the stunned group of fans on the sidewalk.

Cassidy's hand was over her mouth.

Shana's hands were on her hips.

I looked away. I was finished with Shana Fitz.

✳   ✳   ✳

Inside the Hotel Saint Anthony, the security guy sat me down in a little room littered with Styrofoam coffee cups. Five minutes later, a policeman showed up and drove me home in a squad car.

Inside our living room, the cop talked to my parents about "these serious matters." Lizzie took notes with a gel pen and said, "I plan to learn from my big sister's mistakes, Officer."

It was tough keeping my fingernails out of my trap, given the circumstances, but I'm proud to say I didn't nibble on a single digit.

Then Dad sent me to my room. "You'll spend the day there," he said angrily, and grounded me for two weeks. I'd never been grounded in my life. That word hadn't even been in our family vocabulary until now.

A few minutes later, Mom paced back and forth in my room, rattling off all my misdemeanors. Then she paused and shook her head. "I didn't even know you *owned* a jean skirt,

Cat," she said. "Honestly, I feel like I barely recognize you these days."

Then Dad appeared and launched into a lecture, in true professor fashion. He waved a weird-looking piece of paper in the air and said sternly, "I vacuumed this morning, Cat . . . and found *this* under your bed."

Oh *no.* My C- paper! It was all taped together in a mis-shapen mishmash.

I knew the house was a pigsty but whyyyyy did my parents have to pick *today* to clean? And how *could* I have forgotten to throw those bits of paper in the trash can last week?

Dad wiggled the lousy grade for emphasis and said firmly, "You're not to speak with Cassidy on the telephone during these two weeks, Cat. And unless you get your grades up and keep them up, you won't be spending time with her outside of school again."

I looked to Mom for support but she just nodded.

"But you can't separate me from Cassidy for two whole weeks!" I cried. "She's more than just a friend. She's become like a best friend to me."

Dad looked at me and said evenly, "She's not a best friend, Cat, if she doesn't bring out the best in you."

I shook my spiked head and protested, "That C-minus wasn't Cassidy's fault. It was mine. I promise to work harder— but you're wrong about Cassidy. She *does* bring out good things in me! Fun things I never even knew about myself! Just because you both only love classical music and don't care about clothes doesn't mean I have to!"

My parents were quiet for a few minutes. Then my mom took my dad's hand.

"I suppose that's true," she said. "But it will take some getting used to."

"Still, if your grades continue to suffer," my dad added, "you know the consequences. And I'm staying firm—no seeing Cassidy outside of school for two weeks."

Not fair! I huffed and flopped backward onto my pillow.

Then my parents left my room, quietly closing the door behind them.

I sighed. Oh, well. I'd still get to see Cassidy *in* school these next fourteen days. And I'd make sure I'd keep my grades up so I could do stuff with her after that. If she even wanted to do things with me. She might not, after everything Shana had said about me at the limousine that morning. Would Cassidy see there were more sides to this square than just nerdiness?

I fretted about that for a long time, accidentally forgetting about my fingernail resolution. I gnawed two to nubs before I conked out at four o'clock.

I fell sound asleep and slept straight through the night.

The sun woke me up at six-thirty Monday morning, nearly three whole hours before first bell. I decided to e-mail Annie and finally let the *whole* Cat out of the bag. I pecked with my pointer finger:

I know you're still super-busy with school, Annie, but if it's OK with you, I'll just e-scribble some to you. You don't have to write me back until you can. It's just that, well, I have a little extra time on my paws for the next two weeks. . . .

I told her all about the mess I'd gotten myself into, then logged off and headed downstairs for a bowl of granola.

By the time I hoofed it to school, my steps felt soooo heavy that each block was a chore. I knew it wasn't my oversize heels that made my feet drag . . .

. . . it was the fear that Cassidy might be grossed out by the real me.

She was waiting alone at the corner of Murray and Carrey Streets. Shana was nowhere in sight.

I clomped up to her. She kicked at a pile of yellow leaves and didn't even look at me.

Gulp.

Without saying anything, we slowly walked side by side toward school. We crossed the playground and there was Shana—standing at the school door with the horse freaks Billie and Brooke. Shana was wearing her rawhide pants *and* shiny new cowboy boots. Obviously, she was hopping on the hay wagon and joining the cowgirl fashion craze.

Shana waved at Cassidy and called, "Hey, Cass! Come here!"

Cassidy gawked at the cowgirl trio, openmouthed. My heart started to gallop nervously. Oh no, did she want to join the roundup, too? Cassidy would look *so* cute in cowboy boots, and I remembered how much she'd loved Shana's leather pants. . . .

I felt a wave of sadness wash over me. I just knew it was over with Cassidy. Sixth grade without a single girlfriend on American soil. I guessed I'd be eating lunches alone with Greg from now on, enduring all the teasing in the cafeteria. . . .

My eyes started to mist over.

I turned away and trudged through the piles of leaves toward the kindergarten door.

"Cat?"

I stopped and peeked over my shoulder.

Cassidy ran over to me. "How come you're not going through the main entrance?" she asked.

"To *steer* clear of the cowgirl clique," I said firmly. "If I walk past them, I just know I'll get gored by a *bull*."

"By a *bully*, you mean?" Cassidy said. "Shana sure was mean to you yesterday, calling you a geek and practically shaking your head right off your neck."

My heart started to prance like a pony. Could it be? Had Cassidy noticed Shana's mean streak at last? "You mean, you aren't going to join them?"

Cassidy shook her head. "I've had enough."

"Really?" I quickly crossed my arms and legs and wished hard.

"Really. Shana acted totally cranky at the concert last night because she didn't win the dance contest. I spent practically the whole night trying to make her feel better, when all I wanted to do was watch Milo sing! Who needs it? I wish *you'd* been there, Cat."

"Oh!" I squeaked.

"You know, Cat," Cassidy went on, "yesterday at the hotel was the most fun I've had since I moved to St. Paul. Thanks to you."

A great big smile broke out on my face like an exploding star.

But Cassidy's face stayed cloudy. She asked quietly, "Is it true, Cat, the things Shana said about you at the limo?"

I gulped, then stood strong.

I couldn't lie to Cassidy anymore. Or to myself. No more Wimp Girl.

I nodded. "I do get straight A's, Cassidy," I admitted.

Cassidy chewed her lip. Her chin quivered. "If you're so smart," she said in a shaky voice, "why would you want to be friends with me?"

"Because," I said firmly, "you're funny and nice and talented with a hairbrush and a glue gun and you've introduced me to a ton of fun stuff I'd never have tried without you!" I gasped for air.

A slow smile spread over Cassidy's face. She nodded her frizzy head. "So it's settled," she said, and took my arm.

Then the two of us headed into school by way of the kindergarten door. To avoid the bulls in the pasture.

✳ ✳ ✳

Cassidy and I grabbed chairs far away from the cowgirl clique at lunchtime. I was just taking my first bite of tuna sandwich when Greg strolled by our cafeteria table.

"Uh, Cat?" he asked. "Could you help with our science fair project after school today? Data are piling up and I could use some help recording them."

I mumbled, "Sorry, Greg, I can't. I'm, uh, grounded for two weeks."

"You're *grounded*?" Greg exclaimed, totally shocked. "Well, I hope the two weeks go fast, for your sake and mine. I could really use your help with the experiment and . . . it would be nice to see more of you, too, Cat." Greg smiled and stumbled off.

My face grew as warm as my wool sweater. I could feel my cheeks turn my favorite color too—flamingo pink.

Cassidy looked sideways at me and giggled. "What's going on between you and Greg Twitchell?" she demanded with a grin.

I shrugged and took a big chomp of my tuna sandwich. This was *so* embarrassing. . . .

"Well, I'll tell *you* what's going on," Cassidy said. "That boy is driving me crazy. I'd give anything to cut that shaggy hair. I get scissors fever just looking at him!"

And I had a bad case of boy fever. Oh my gosh!

✴   ✴   ✴

The next morning at school, I spied a huge swarm of girls on the playground. I marched through the dry leaves toward the huddle.

"What's happening?" I asked a fifth-grade girl.

"Have you *seen* him?" the girl breathed. "He is soooo cute. He's got the dreamiest, biggest blue eyes and the most adorable face."

A girl from 6C gushed, "He's my new crush. Forget Milo Lennox!"

"Who's your new crush?" I asked.

Suddenly Cassidy leaped over to me and cried, "I told Greg I'd help him with his science fair project after school while you're grounded! I know you like him, Cat, I can tell. And any friend of yours is a friend of mine. I don't take fab notes but I can watch those gauge thingies and I just love wearing those funky safety goggles! Anyhow, Greg said he really needed my help and soooo . . . I said I'd do it . . . *if* he let me put my scissors to work. Greg thought about it, then finally he said he was tired of buckling under Judd the Jerk. And he let me!"

"You mean, *you cut his hair*?" I gasped.

I pushed forward through the crowd . . . and there was Greg at the center, looking sheepish and exceedingly cute without his sheepdog fringe. He had a small crop of curls and huge blue eyes that were knocking the neon socks off all the schoolgirls. Including Shana, who stood staring at him, speechless.

Just then, Judd the Jerk shot out of nowhere and started to torment Greg. "Twitchell's got—" But before he could finish, a pack of girls grabbed him and buried him under a pile of leaves.

Cassidy giggled, then turned around and studied me a minute. She picked up a strand of my stringy hair and said, "You know, a short radical cut would look *really* cute on you, too, Cat. You're next!"

I wrinkled my nose, smiled and said, "Hmm . . . *maybe*."

About the Author

SHELLEY SWANSON SATEREN has worked as an editor, bookseller and freelance writer and is the author of several nonfiction books for young readers. Growing up, she was always the new girl in school.

Shelley Swanson Sateren lives in St. Paul, Minnesota, with her husband and two young sons and loves both classical and contemporary music. *Cat on a Hottie's Tin Roof* is her first novel.